WALDMEER SERIES

COMBINED VOLUME BOOKS 1 TO 2

A SPIRITUAL FICTION SERIES

DONNA GODDARD

Second Edition 2023

Published by Donna Goddard

Victoria, Australia

Paperback ISBN: 978-0645729672

Cover design by Donna Goddard

www.donnagoddard.com

CONTENTS

WALDMEER SERIES

COMBINED VOLUME BOOKS 1 TO 2

Waldmeer (Book 1)
Together (Book 2)

WALDMEER (BOOK 1)

PART I
IN WALDMEER

SPIRIT ON EARTH

THE GARDEN

CHAPTER 1
ONE WHO SPEAKS

In the spirit world of a garden on Earth:

The gardener walked into their lives bright and sharp. A ready smile covered her need. She came from a house with walls that echoed loneliness. On the very first day, her eyes were drawn to the little flower in the corner of the garden. Its beauty was in its simplicity. The gardener's jealousy was already born. She watched it every day. It moved to the breeze and reached for the sunshine. The flower did not complain about the dark, the wind, or the cold. Its roots had strength unseen.

The little flower was called Amira. Farkas, the garden spirit, guarded her. He loved Amira most of all the garden residents. However, he was wounded. He had lived many lives and carried the damage inside himself. He often went away, and they would not see him for long periods. Sometimes, he would sit near Amira and remember things he rarely let himself remember. He would rest there until the wind called him away again.

The gardener watched it all, and her loathing grew darker.

How can the little flower have such a hold over the garden spirit's heart? she thought.

One morning, before the rising light had given its blessing to the day, the gardener, sick with her longing, left her bed and killed the little flower.

Now, Farkas will learn to love me, she thought. *He will come to look at me and feel alive. He will protect me instead of the pathetic, dead flower.*

When Farkas next returned, he went to greet Amira. He had missed his sweet friend. His eyes filled with rage when he saw that his little love was gone. He knew instantly what had happened and stormed to the gardener with fire and death in his breath. The gardener was frightened.

"I only wanted you to love me," she said.

"You cannot kill another being and then claim their spirit as your own," he spat at her. "I despise you."

Still, he let her stay in the garden.

She reminded him that he hated life.

He wanted to hate life.

Despite Farkas's disgust for her, the gardener still longed for him. She waited for his return, but the absences became longer until he barely returned at all. When he did, he gave her nothing of his essence.

The garden became a soulless place. It had no nourishment. One day, the gardener realised that if she stayed any longer, she too would be consumed by the slow death.

And so, she left.

She did not say goodbye.

She did not wish to prolong the pain.

THE GARDEN WAS VERY STILL. A gentle breeze moved through the silent trees. It stirred the long, dry grass. A lone bird landed on a high branch. Surprisingly, it stayed there. Farkas was far away, but he sensed that something had changed. He could feel a quickening movement in his soul. He returned to the garden and looked around. Not much was alive.

Nevertheless, there was a subtle, sweet scent that had not been there before. In the place where the little flower had once lived, a tiny seed had sprouted and was holding onto earth and air with all its might. It was willing itself to grow into a strong and beautiful flower again. It looked so fragile. Fragility is the mask of mastery.

"I will stay here," Farkas called to the distant wind. "The garden needs me."

CHAPTER 2

THE GUILTLESS GARDEN

*I*n the inter-dimensional Garden of Garourinn in the North Country:

The gardener, Verloren, left in despair. Leaving was painful, but staying would have been worse. She carried the guilt of murder—and the darker guilt of having wanted to consume another being.

After several weeks of travel that seemed to be going nowhere, she remembered a bedtime story her grandfather had told her as a small child.

Verloren, when you are weary, go to the Garden of Garourinn. It is in the North Country, where the winters are long and cold. You will find the Head Gardener there if you are so fortunate to be graced by his presence.

It was the first clear idea that Verloren had had in a long time.

Go quickly, girl, she thought she heard her grandfather add. *The season has not yet turned, and you will be able to cross to the North Country. If you wait any longer, the pass will freeze, and you will indeed wait a long time until it is clear again.*

She set off immediately, feeling that no other option was any less arduous. While travelling, she pondered with surprise and relief that her grandfather's voice seemed to hold no reproach.

Perhaps, she thought, *he doesn't know what I have done.*

She pushed the thought out of her mind, being sure it was the case. Just as her grandfather said, the pass was not yet frozen. With considerable effort, often having to retrace her steps from wrong turns, she made it to the other side, tired but unharmed.

She glanced back at the pass. Winter was nearly upon it. If she did not find Garourinn quickly, she would not cross again until spring.

The days went by. Not only could she not find Garourinn, but everyone she asked gave different answers. Some said it was a myth, and she was wasting her time. Some said it was high in the mountains but near impossible to find. Some insisted they had just come from it and that it was only up the road. She followed each direction. There was no garden.

The last day was upon her, and she had to make her way back to the pass before it closed. Her mission had failed, and she had nothing to return to that was worth living for. Perhaps it would be better to walk so slowly that the pass did freeze...

Verloren was startled by a sudden voice.

Don't be foolish, girl, said her grandfather. *Do you think that going to sleep will end your pain? It will not. Climb the next hill on your left, and you will find Garourinn.*

Wide awake and with hope in her heart, Verloren reached the crest of the hill. The view stole her breath.

Perhaps I have already died, she thought.

She seemed alive, so she walked down into the green valley, starkly contrasting the surrounding mountains of white, rocky ice. There were trees, grassy meadows, and little homes. Everything looked peaceful. The sun was somehow shining warmly on this valley only. The massive walls of cold mountain were forbidding, yet they acted as a protection for the valley without infringing on its microcosm.

Stopping at one of the little cottages because the door was ajar, Verloren entered and felt immediately at home. A fire was sharing soft, comforting light with the room. She realised that she was freezing, wet, and starving. There were clean, dry clothes on a chair. They seemed to belong to her, although they were much simpler than her typical taste in fashion. She gratefully took off her wet clothes and pulled the new ones on. Strangely, she had never felt so beautiful in any clothing she had ever bought.

Warm bread, creamy butter, fragrant cheese, and slices of red apple were on the table. A sweet lemon and orange drink was more delicious than anything Verloren had ever tasted. Feeling safe and content, she lay on the welcoming bed and instantly fell deeply asleep. She did not have a worry in the world and could not even recall why anyone could possibly be worried about anything.

The morning light made dancing patterns on the floor. Verloren woke and suddenly remembered her quest. Having found the Garden of Garourinn, she must now find the Head Gardener. She recalled that there were things she wanted, and this was her chance to get them. The memory quickened her pulse.

Not seeing anyone to ask directions, she hastily walked back to the top of the hill to get a better view. She turned to the pass and saw that it had almost frozen over. On turning back to Garourinn, she saw, to her horror, that the garden valley was there no more.

Hurry, Verloren, the icy wind said as it swirled around her. *You have no more time. Run to the pass and cross now. You will not find Garourinn here again.*

Verloren ran to the pass, managed to cross it, and, on reaching the other side, fell to the ground in a sheltered place. She slept, exhausted and troubled. The following day, still utterly exhausted and unable to move, she tried to make sense of her journey.

What a complete failure, she thought. *All I got was one strange moment of peace that vanished as quickly as it came.*

The hours passed as she walked, but the bleakness did not.

Perhaps my grandfather will talk to me again, she thought.

Presently, his gentle voice floated into the recesses of her mind, moving in and then vanishing as soon as she concentrated on it.

If I relax, she thought, *I may hear him better.*

The voice became more audible, and Verloren realised it was not her grandfather's.

"I am the one you sought," said the voice. "I am the Head Gardener. You are not ready to see me. Still, you did well. You found the Garden, if only for a moment. The healing you received will help you become lighter.

Garourinn is my home. It is yours as well. Now that you have made the treacherous journey once, try to find it in your sleep. Each visit will strengthen you.

You carry guilt, as most on Earth do. Here, there is none. Those who visit start to see their real form—whole and beautiful.

By the way, I know your grandfather well. He has been here many times, but now he walks other lands."

CHAPTER 3
DON'T COME BACK

In the spirit world of the Waldmeer garden:

Farkas tried to keep the little flower alive, but it was not going well. He wanted to settle in the garden, but was restless and distracted.

"I am not feeling well," said the little flower, Amira, softly one evening.

"You are so strong," said Farkas, looking worried.

"Make yourself well again," he commanded as if such a thing could be commanded.

"When I am a flower," Amira explained, "I rely on those who care for me. I cannot change that. I think you should go to the Homeland for a while. It is autumn here, and we will all survive without you for the coming months."

In the inter-dimensional Homeland:

When Farkas arrived at the Homeland, he was sent to the Vastandamine Forest and told to rest there. He went, but he could not rest. He knew the forest's talent. It brought forward whatever needed healing most. No one ever wanted to go there, yet everyone knew its value.

Sure enough, before long, he had a visitor. It was his last Earth father. The likeness was uncomfortably apparent. Neither said anything. After a week of occasional appearances, Farkas's temper got the better of him.

"What the hell are you doing here?" he demanded. "Do you think I want to see you?" His eyes narrowed and grew dark. "If so, you are dead wrong."

His father looked neither apologetic nor offended, nor as if he intended to leave.

"You never showed the slightest interest in us," continued Farkas. "Fuck off, and don't come back."

Upon his father's departure, Farkas felt a sense of victory and also a strange disappointment.

Couldn't he, at least, explain himself? he thought. *Better still, say sorry. For God's sake, say sorry.*

One evening, as Farkas walked by the river, he saw his father's reflection in the water.

I told him to go, he thought.

He swung around, insults ready. Nobody was there, but the reflection still was. He looked more closely and was shocked to see it was his own reflection.

It is disturbing enough to hold a lifelong grudge against another person. It is much worse to realise that the person is oneself.

The grip of anger was loosening, and sorrow was taking its place. Farkas had cried many times for himself but rarely about himself. That would have been too confronting.

A woman appeared and spoke reassuringly to him as if none of this mattered.

"I am Milyaket, Keeper of the Forest," she said. "Your time with us is done. Come with me, please."

Disliking the forest intensely, Farkas followed her. He had nothing to say that was worth saying, so he let Milyaket's soothing voice continue its rhythmic speech.

"We know you are in pain," said Milyaket. "You blame others to avoid attacking yourself, but neither is necessary. You are not as you think, nor is anyone else."

Farkas could not help but soften to Milyaket. She was so calm, peaceful, and good. He saw none of himself in her. That helped. He wanted to keep his forest discovery a secret. Besides, he did not even understand what it all meant.

Milyaket spoke as if she were a consented part of Farkas's thought conversation.

"Anything held in secret cannot be healed," she said. "The light cannot reach that which is locked away in the dark."

They reached a large, open room. Farkas could see very little, but Milyaket acted as if there were things and people everywhere.

"The Advisors have convened," said Milyaket. "They suggest that you return to Earth in human form to continue your journey. They feel that you will make better progress with a body."

"I love a creature that is a spirit," said Farkas. "If I return as a human, we will be too different to connect."

It was the only time he spoke.

"You see the separation of life as very arbitrary at this time," said Milyaket. "You are not alone in this assumption. You have far more connection than you are even vaguely aware of. You will not lose the love that is yours. Return now."

In Waldmeer:

The garden was asleep. It was early winter. Farkas's stride was sure and grounded. Dark hair. A well-proportioned body. A self-contained face. Eyes that were both soft and hard.

"It doesn't feel bad to be human," said Farkas. "Let's try this again."

CHAPTER 4
WINTER'S OVER

In Waldmeer:

Winter was coming to a close. Farkas was getting used to being back in a body. He had spent the last few months doing simple tasks and thinking. He looked forward to spring because the warmth would bring the garden back to life. That meant that his little flower friend, Amira, would wake up. He had so much to tell her.

She would be surprised that he now had a body. He hoped she liked his new body. He glanced into the pond to assess it from a flower's point of view. He couldn't tell. Who would know what a flower thinks?

Much of the garden had already awoken and was spreading in all directions. Farkas kept looking at the spot where his favourite friend lived to see if there were any signs of life.

Strange, he thought. *I can't remember Amira being a late grower. A* terrible thought crossed his mind. *She isn't asleep. She's dead. She's not coming back.*

Farkas reassured himself with the memory that she had restarted her life as a tiny seed once before.

She will do that again, he thought.

She didn't. This time, she didn't come back.

THE SUMMER DAYS were long and warm. There was always a late afternoon sea breeze to sweep away the remaining heat. Everyone in the little town slept with their windows open. The waves, the stars, and the morning birds were the bedmates of all who lived in the village.

Farkas had recently invited another bedmate into his home. Her name was Elise.

It did not take long for the village girls to realise that there was a new resident in the cottage on the hill. He was reserved, masculine, striking, and seemed entirely single.

Elise, the village's prettiest and most confident girl, marked him as hers. The other girls knew not to challenge her. She had a young, sleek body, long blonde hair, and an infectious smile. Her conversation style was bright and flippant.

At first, Farkas was not interested. However, he soon decided it was ridiculous to grieve over a flower spirit, no matter how close they had been.

For God's sake, he thought. *She was a flower. Anyway, she is gone and isn't coming back.*

Besides, he had forgotten that along with a male body comes the drive for a womanly one. Elise was very willing to be that womanly body. And so, Farkas lost himself in her.

It was certainly fun. He even managed to forget his problems somewhat. He started to play with the idea that it might be maintainable and bring him happiness. He reached towards her warm, sleeping body and drew it closer. Elise responded obediently, although she was completely asleep.

Farkas could not help feeling two conflicting ways about her.

One was simple, gratuitous pleasure. The other was dislike. He didn't like her. It crossed his mind that he had never felt conflicted about Amira. She loved him purely, and he responded with instinctive devotion. Amira was the only place he felt no conflict. He liked being with her.

As for Elise? He liked her body. He liked her smell. He liked her submissive adoration. Nothing about her scared him. Nothing challenged him. He also found her boring, needy, and shallow. She did not love him. She needed him. Her loyalty was to her survival.

Farkas knew he was no better. He struggled to find enough love to give to himself, let alone someone else. Yet, he thought there must be something inside him because he could love Amira. That love came from somewhere.

His memory of Amira and his previous life was fading fast. Now that he had a human body, it was surprising he remembered his spirit life at all. The memories lingered, but not for long.

After that day with Elise, Farkas could not bring himself to invite her into the house again. Even if he could not have love, he did not have to choose some meaningless, second-rate version of it. It was better to be alone. A few months later, he happened to pass Elise on the street. She didn't see him. She was too busy laughing with her new companion, looking into his eyes as if he were God.

Yes, thought Farkas, *it's better to be alone.*

MARIA OF WALDMEER

CHAPTER 5

A GIFT FROM GOD

In Waldmeer:

Lenny was a fisherman from Waldmeer. His family had lived in the coastal village for generations. A German ancestor had first settled there as a logger, in a place where forest met the sea.

At seventeen, Lenny built the small fibro cottage he and his wife would always live in. It was simple and well cared for, with an unpretentious garden, an orchard heavy with fruit for jam, hens scratching at the bottom of the slope, and a vegetable patch that had fed the family for decades. Their life was steady and unambitious. Until a few days ago.

They were now sitting in the country hospital, anxious and weary. With nerves on edge, they were waiting to see what would happen to Maria, their sixteen-year-old daughter. She had been in intensive care for three days. The unthinkable had happened, and she was hit by the school bus on its daily trek along the long, winding coastal road. Her parents' only consolation was that Maria had become immediately unconscious, so they felt she was not in pain.

Many years ago, they had been told that they would not be able to have children. Maria was a wonderful surprise after fifteen years of marriage. They said she was a gift from God—when they would allow themselves such sentimentalities.

Maria was an unusually sweet child with not a mean bone in her body. Her goals in life were simple. She was happy to go to school and help her mother in the small cafe she managed in Waldmeer. Maria was always pleasant to the customers, perhaps a bit dreamy at times, but delightful. She was a genuine asset to the business. She used her earnings to buy small gifts for friends and to save for her future. Now it seemed she would not have one.

"I am so sorry," said the doctor-in-charge, summoning all his professional training as he entered the hospital room. "I do not think Maria will live past this evening. It is probably best to say your goodbyes."

In the inter-dimensional Homeland:

Maria had almost completely transitioned to the Homeland. As her parents had hoped, she felt no pain at all. Her main concern was that her parents might not be as calm about her leaving as she was.

"Don't worry about your parents," said Maria's inter-dimensional guardian, reassuringly. "It has all been taken care of."

Amira had been given access to this whole Earth drama unfolding. She saw the accident and watched Maria's guardians look after her as she moved out of her body. They talked to Maria calmly, and there was little stress in the situation for her, despite the great deal of stress in the human world.

Milyaket, Keeper of the Forest, approached Amira.

"We have been so enjoying having you back in the Homeland,"

said Milyaket, "but, like all of us, you know that in helping others, you find greater happiness yourself."

Amira nodded. She had learned that lesson a long time ago. In the Homeland, where there were many advanced beings, she was frequently reminded how much she still had to learn.

"The Advisors would like to ask you if you are willing to return to Earth in the body of young Maria," Milyaket continued. "She is a suitable match for you, and you will not find her past life or tendencies too grating."

"Of course," said Amira, knowing that whatever the Advisors suggested was always in one's best interest.

"There is one more thing you must know," Milyaket added. "Once you have entered Maria's body, you will not be able to recall your life as you know it now. You will remember Maria's life as if it were your own. Her memory and demeanour will gradually transform into your own consciousness. This way, you and Maria's parents will adjust to the change."

In Waldmeer:

Lenny and his wife could not believe their blessed good fortune when, in the early evening, Maria started to move her arms and open her eyes. She was returning to them.

"Tomorrow," said Lenny for the first and only time ever. "I would like to go to the chapel."

CHAPTER 6

WALDMEER CORNER
STORE AND CAFE

Maria's progress was rapid and steady. Everyone in Waldmeer and the surrounding towns knew of the accident and the girl's unexpected recovery. She was soon well enough to do short shifts in the cafe her mother managed, Waldmeer Corner Store and Cafe. It was agreed that it would be best for her to do her remaining year of schooling from home. The townsfolk did not speak to Maria about the accident in case it drew attention to something that might pull her backwards. Instead, they spoke in hushed tones to Maria's mother.

Farkas was one of the morning coffee visitors to the cafe. He always got takeaway as he couldn't be bothered with other people's annoying civilities. He could barely remember Maria before the accident, but even he was curious about the girl's miraculous recovery. He looked at her closely to see if she really was okay. He was a little embarrassed to find that something about the girl was interesting.

Over the coming year, Farkas gradually started having his coffee at the cafe tables. He would read the paper and sometimes talk briefly with Maria's mother, who was not much older than he was. Maria would smile at him when she cleared his table, although she was a bit nervous about the man who lived on the hill. No one in the village seemed to know anything about him, where he came from, how long he was there for, or even what work he did. Farkas certainly wasn't telling anyone anything.

Occasionally, one of the hill-dwellers would ask Maria if she could remember anything from when she was unconscious. Curious to know the answer but too conservative to ask, others would stop talking and listen for the reply. Maria didn't want to disappoint anyone, but could remember nothing.

Happy birthday, Maria, Farkas heard one of the cafe regulars say one morning.

"Is it your birthday?" he asked when she brought his coffee. "How old are you?"

The question sounded more important than he intended.

"Eighteen," said Maria.

And something about that answer made Farkas happier than he felt it should have.

MARIA WAS CHANGING. Her parents noticed it and felt it must be a result of the accident. They didn't question her about it as they were grateful to have her with them in any form. Farkas noticed it, too.

She was beginning to look older. Perhaps it was the normal change from girl to woman, but it seemed more than that. Her eyes looked like they were searching for something. Previously, Maria never had that look on her face. It was not the restlessness of young adulthood that pushes the person from the safety of home out into the world's adventure. If it were that, Maria would have been outgrowing the cafe and dreaming of the city. She was content with her work in Waldmeer Corner Store and Cafe.

It was a different kind of restlessness. It was the restlessness that comes from inside when one cannot quite remember what one is here to do.

Farkas also noticed that he was not the only person with a growing interest in Maria. Charlie lived in the back hills of Wald-meer. She was about ten years older than Maria and ten years younger than Farkas. Her real name was Charmaine, but no one called her that.

She had very short, almost shaved, black hair and large, dark eyes that were as intense as Farkas's. She wasn't masculine, nor was she feminine. She was unapologetically androgynous. This woman knew what she was doing. She was an up-and-coming artist who already had works in some of the city's galleries. She was unpretentious and treated everyone the same, except for people who annoyed her.

She seemed to sense something unusual in Maria, and Farkas could see that Charlie was nurturing it and her. This troubled him. He could not tell what Charlie wanted with Maria.

He knew how to deal with men. You make them feel nervous about challenging you, and they will respect your territory. Women? You flirt with them just enough for them to think you have an interest in them, and then you leave them wanting more. What do you do with someone who thinks differently, comes at things from a different angle, and won't engage in the conflict? Maria liked Charlie. She felt Charlie might have answers to questions she couldn't even form properly.

To add to Farkas's perceived problem, Charlie often came into the cafe with one of her long-term friends, Gabriel. Gabriel was also an artist. He lived in the city and used Charlie's Waldmeer house for sculpting at various times of the year. Charlie and Gabriel were well known and respected in Waldmeer, which was no small achievement given the traditional nature of small country towns.

It was common knowledge that Gabriel had had both male and female partners. Unlike Charlie, he was not androgynous. He was very much a man. Both Charlie and Gabriel had an emotional freedom and courage that Maria was drawn to.

In turn, they sensed the spirit in Maria. After all, they were artists. And artists see the invisible before anyone else.

CHAPTER 7
ERDO KAPUS

Maria spent a lot of time in the back hills of Waldmeer. She visited Charlie at her art studio and Gabriel when he was there. Charlie knew a lot about life and people and was generous in sharing it.

"You are too young to know this," Charlie said one afternoon, "but relationships are full of problems. We are drawn to them as if they are the great treasure of life, yet we struggle once we are in them. Those who say otherwise are lying."

She paused and said more kindly, "Not that it's a bad lie, but it's a lie."

As if to redirect her train of thought, Charlie added, "Erdo says that we must try to tell ourselves whenever we feel distressed about our relationships, 'There is another way of looking at this.' What do you think?"

"Who is Erdo?" asked Maria.

"Erdo Kapus. He is my teacher," said Charlie. "He lives in the Leleks."

"What sort of a teacher?"

"The only teacher that matters."

"Who does he teach?"

"Anyone who looks for him."

"In the forest?"

"Yes, the Leleks."

"Does he have a family?"

"No, he is old and lives alone. He says he has a sister, Milyaket, but I have never seen her."

Milyaket? thought Maria.

A memory stirred, but it was so far away that she had no hope of gathering it.

"Has Gabriel ever been to see Erdo?" asked Maria.

"No," said Charlie, "but I often tell him what Erdo tells me. Gabriel and I have a joke when we think someone is being egotistical. 'That's ego, not Erdo.' It's a lame joke, but we both find it funny for some reason. I don't think Gabriel believes everything I tell him, but he always listens."

"Can you take me to see Erdo?" asked Maria. "Will he see me?"

"I will take you," said Charlie, "but it's not for me to say who he will see."

"Will you tell him I would like to come," asked Maria.

"There is no need to tell him," said Charlie. "He will know. He will either be there or not."

IN THE LELEKS:

The following week, Charlie drove Maria an hour into the Leleks, the large forested area behind Waldmeer. Erdo lived in a part of the forest that was not a national park, but no one else seemed to own it. It was slow driving because the dirt track was bumpy and windy, even though it wasn't that far. Charlie parked the car at the narrow walking bridge.

"Aren't you coming?" asked Maria.

"No, he only likes one person to visit at a time," said Charlie. "He says it's less distracting for us. Walk over the hill. If he is coming, he will be there."

He wasn't there. Maria sat on a log by the pond and listened to the birds.

"What would you like to ask?" said a voice behind her.

She turned to see who had spoken. Erdo was supposedly old, but he looked like he could be any age over forty. Suddenly, Maria could not think of one single question worth asking. Erdo was so still that there didn't seem to be anything important enough to ask that would be worth breaking the silence for. It was Erdo himself who spoke in the manner of continuing a conversation that had started a long time ago.

"Everything that comes from this world is problematic," he said. "That is because this world is the upside-down of the real world. It is a suffering one. I will give you a choice today. If you prefer, you can leave and go gently into the real world, and there you will be spared much suffering, and you will only feel happiness. Think carefully. Your choice will determine your path."

Erdo left her at the pond and said he would return soon. The pond was idyllic. Everything was glowing with light and beauty, and so profoundly peaceful that it was inconceivable that anything could take away from the gorgeous bliss.

Who would not want this? thought Maria.

She became increasingly unaware of her body and felt merged with all the living things around her. She was fast losing awareness of who she was in that other tiny, dysfunctional world of strange bodies fighting with themselves and each other.

After some time, Maria saw two spectacular black swans land balletically on the pond and swim harmoniously amongst the water lilies. They were not asking anything from each other, yet they were together.

People are so separate in that other little world, thought Maria.

"The darkness uses relationships to keep people revolving around the ego's demands," said Erdo, who had returned.

"If relationships cause people so much angst and heartbreak," said Maria, "wouldn't it be better to forget about them and only think of the real world?"

"In the beginning, people see the beauty of the divine in each other," explained Erdo. "They are captivated and delighted by it, but quickly forget what they once saw as fear reclaims its supremacy. So begins the fight to protect oneself and one's rightful claims. What is owed becomes paramount. Guilt becomes the preferred tool of manipulation. Freedom is lost in the battle. Love is forgotten. What is left are the rare moments of peace and forgiveness, which somehow save the day."

Erdo cheerfully turned to Maria and said, "And what will it be? Are you staying or going?"

Maria couldn't help feeling that Erdo knew the answer, but he was waiting for a reply.

"Seeing as I am already here, I will stay," said Maria. "Maybe someone needs me."

"Many need you." Erdo smiled warmly. "And you need them. We do not get to Heaven alone. Charlie is waiting for you on the other side of the bridge. You have kept her waiting long enough."

"We don't want her getting angry," he added as if Charlie were a naughty puppy.

~

IN WALDMEER:

A few days later, in the cafe, Maria overheard two locals talking about the old man and his recent sightings in the Leleks.

"Yeah, right, in ya' dreams, mate," both laughed with the good-natured superiority that keeps mates together 'cause they know better.

"Have you ever seen the old man who lives in the forest, Farkas?" Maria ventured.

"Yeah, I have," said Farkas.

Maria was surprised.

"I've seen him a few times when I've been near the old bridge," said Farkas.

"Have you spoken to him?"

"He gestured to me, both times I've seen him, to cross the bridge."

"And did you?" asked Maria.

"Of course not. I don't trust him," Farkas snapped angrily.

He pushed his chair out, almost knocking Maria over.

Maria wanted to cry, but couldn't because she was at work.

As for Farkas, he stopped coming to the cafe.

THE LELEKS

CHAPTER 8
FAMILY

Ever since Farkas stormed out of the cafe, not to return, Maria felt ill. She was even finding some of the cafe customers annoying. Mrs Reisenden was one of them. Maria's mother liked her and enjoyed talking with her whenever she visited Waldmeer.

"You have returned," said Maria's mother with obvious delight. "Do tell me how life has been in the city since you last were here on holiday."

Mrs Reisenden would often bring Maria's mother a little present, and she would tell her all about the cultural events she had been attending.

"Maria, dear, please bring Verloren's coffee over," said Maria's mother. "I will sit here and chat with her as we haven't had the pleasure of her company for a while."

She turned to Verloren and said, "This morning, I walked past the old cottage on the hill. I recalled that several summers ago, you did some gardening work there. They were so lucky to have you!"

"You are too kind," said Verloren.

Verloren had mixed memories of her time at the house but could not recall exactly why.

"Does it have a new person living there now?" said Verloren. "I must introduce myself to them."

Mrs Reisenden must have been the gardener at Farkas's house before he moved in, thought Maria.

"I enjoyed my time at that house," said Verloren. "It was good to do some manual gardening again. We have to keep grounded, you know. We can't be high and mighty."

Maria gave Mrs Reisenden her coffee. As she turned away from Verloren, she rolled her eyes. Maria loved her mother, but the difference in their tastes was becoming markedly wider.

In the Leleks:

As Maria was still not feeling well, she decided to visit Erdo.

"Your body would not get sick if you held no thought of resentment," said Erdo, as if this were elementary knowledge. "It is neither good nor bad in itself. If you use it to bless, it will not complain. If we hold anything against anyone, we will suffer ourselves."

That is not easy, but perhaps I could take it on board, thought Maria. *At least I wouldn't feel sick anymore, so it's probably worth it.*

"More than this," continued Erdo, "you are the very people you dislike."

"I am not those people," said Maria.

"I am not those people," she repeated, a fire rising inside her. "I am not Farkas with his stupid, angry attitude pushing everyone away as if they all want to kill him. I am not that bare-boobed girl, Elise, running around town sleeping with anyone she thinks she can get something from. I am not that woman from the city, Verloren Reisenden. She acts like she is so kind, but she lies to her husband, chases good-looking men, and spends her time shopping and talking to her friends about how badly life is treating her. Those women come together under the guise of love to gossip about people who have what they do not. And if they cannot pull someone into their suffering, they turn on them."

Erdo remained silent for some time and then said, "You are all those people. If one is left behind, none of us gets there. No one can be forgotten. We are one creation. We are family. Whoever you hold accountable for their mistaken identity holds you in the dream."

That's too hard, thought Maria.

"If it were too hard, you would not be hearing this now," said Erdo. "We hear what we are ready to hear. We draw into our lives those who will help us grow. We tend to have mixed feelings about them, but they are marked for us. We invited them into our house and forgot that we wrote the invitation. We look at them as intruders when all along they are guests."

In Waldmeer:

Maria bumped into Farkas a few days later while walking to the shops.

"Hello, Maria," said Farkas, who acted like there was no reason not to be friendly.

Maybe he wants something, thought Maria.

"I hear you are spending a lot of time in the hills with Charlie?" said Farkas.

"Yes," said Maria. "I am with Gabriel as much as Charlie. Charlie and I talk about Erdo, the old man in the forest. Gabriel and I talk about life."

Maria was being far more generous with information about her private life than she felt she should be.

"Gabriel? The gay guy from the city?" asked Farkas.

"Yes," said Maria. "Do you know him?"

Farkas nodded that he knew him, but looked like he did not want to know him any more than he already did. There didn't seem to be anything Maria could say to divert a conversation headed nowhere good.

Farkas turned to leave.

"By the way," he added, "a lady, Verloren, called in at my house. She said she used to do gardening there before I moved in. She also said she would call again."

Call again? Maria thought. *It is surprising Farkas let her call once.*

"She comes to the cafe," said Maria. "My mother likes her. Erdo says I must like her too."

"Are you sure that's what he meant?" Farkas asked. "The woman, Verloren, said gardening was good for her because it made her forget about herself and her problems."

That was honest of Mrs Reisenden, Maria thought. *It was strange of Farkas to have such a conversation with her. He hardly spoke to anyone, let alone someone like her.*

For a moment, Maria and Farkas looked at each other as if both were trying to recollect things they could not recall: invisible bonds and an unclear purpose. As neither could remember, they returned to their usual demeanour and said goodbye.

CHAPTER 9
HOLD MY HAND

G abriel was a relatively free thinker. He wasn't one of those gay guys who acted like a stupid girl — preening, gossiping, catty, shallow, forever parading their latest drama.

He was not on remote control, chasing marriage, mortgage, and children in the hope that the masses might know what they were doing. He might not have answers, but he had questions. Perhaps that was why he was an artist. He looked for answers in his art.

He mostly worked as a sculptor and was used to using his hands. They were interesting hands—purposeful like a carpenter, but soft like a musician.

Sometimes, he took Maria's hand as they walked along Merri Creek through Charlie's hillside property. As he was generally affectionate, it felt natural enough, and neither said anything about it. They simply walked—listening to the wind, watching the water, talking calmly about life.

It made Maria think about the body and how we connect through touch.

In the back hills:

"Oh, don't ask me that," said Charlie when Maria asked her what she thought was the best approach to sex. "I have had problems in all my relationships."

Maria sensed Charlie was about to launch into a long account of those problems.

"What does Erdo say?" she asked quickly.

Charlie shifted her attention. "He says we use sex to try to complete ourselves—because we feel fragmented."

That doesn't sound very encouraging, thought Maria.

"He also says we're drawn to people who seem to have what we lack. We think if we unite with them, we'll gain it."

Oh, that sounds even worse, thought Maria.

"Does he say anything good about it?" asked Maria.

"Yes," said Charlie. "He says even though our relationships begin selfishly, they can become our saviour. Through them, we come to see ourselves, the other person, and life more clearly. 'Offer your relationships to God,' he says, 'and you won't be disappointed with what is made of them.'"

Most people want to use sex for their own purposes, Maria thought, *not be used by it for a purpose other than their own. Life is tricky. Maybe it is not so much deceptive as it is wise and kind, and knows how to get our attention.*

That thought satisfied her, and she felt it was a direction worth heading towards.

In Waldmeer:

Not long after, Maria met Gabriel for coffee while he was in town. They avoided her workplace, Waldmeer Corner Store and

Cafe. There was only one other decent cafe in Waldmeer. Since Farkas no longer went to Maria's cafe, he now got his coffee there —and happened to be walking out just as Maria and Gabriel walked in.

"Hello, Farkas. You know Gabriel, of course," said Maria cheerfully.

The air thickened.

"How are things in the city with the boys?" asked Farkas, the edge unmistakable.

Gabriel lifted his eyebrows and replied slowly, "Yeah, good, thanks. How about you, Farkas?" — pronouncing it Fuckarse.

Oh my God, thought Maria. *That's a red flag to a bull. This is getting serious.*

Neither man was paying her the slightest attention now. They were far more interested in insulting each other. And suddenly it struck her as funny. She laughed.

Both men looked at her, startled and annoyed, as if to say, *Why are you even standing there? And, anyway, you're really too weird sometimes.*

Nevertheless, the tension had been broken.

"I don't know why I was given such a ridiculous name," Farkas said at last, a reluctant smile breaking through. "I have enough trouble in life without fighting every Tom, Dick, and Harry for my dignity."

Maria took the opportunity to leave her two friends. "I'll catch you later, Gabriel."

Halfway down the street she glanced back. The two men were still there, talking — cautiously.

Perhaps not best friends, she thought, *but with the respect that is due.*

CHAPTER 10

NIGHTMARE

I t had been raining all week in Waldmeer. Some of the roads had closed due to landslides, and there was mud every-where. Maria had been having nightmares.

On the way to see Erdo, she had a foreboding feeling, which was made worse by his not being there when she arrived. She crossed the rampaging river and climbed the hill from which Erdo usually appeared.

The forest was getting darker.

It must be going to rain again, Maria thought.

The nightmare started creeping in.

Sensing it, she walked more slowly until her footsteps were silent as she moved carefully through the trees, lest she offend the approaching enemy.

Maria didn't want to continue, but going back seemed as daunting as going forward.

As soon as she reached the top of the hill, she stopped dead in her tracks.

A dense and terrible power was rising from the valley.

It was back—and far worse than before.

It felt like all the evil in the world and more.

She felt it intended to sweep her up effortlessly and, with barely a glance, crush every bone in her body and drop her to die painfully below.

Terror immobilised both her body and mind.

Wake up, she heard herself say.

This time, there was no waking up because she wasn't asleep.

She was a tiny leaf about to be brutally crushed.

As the pressure from the monster was closing in on her, a distant memory called from deep within her.

Maria, it is I, said a female voice. *I am with you. I know this monster. It is defeatable. Listen to me. You made the monster. Now unmake it.*

The voice was familiar, yet Maria didn't know who it was. At this point, it didn't matter.

"Unmake it? How? It's crushing me," said Maria.

Stand your ground. Do not close your eyes. Look at it, said the voice.

Maria looked. It was horrible: suffering and pain.

Look deeper, said the voice. *It is the world you have all made. It is only a nightmare.*

As Maria looked more closely, her terror started to soften.

Let it be blown away as nothing, said the voice. *I am here waiting for you.*

"Let it be blown away as nothing. I am here waiting for you," repeated Maria.

The darkness began to fracture.

Maria's body was no longer under pressure.

The trees were becoming visible.

The sun started to glisten on the wet leaves.

A sense of harmony, peace, and safety settled over her.

Maria felt it would be impossible for anything ever to hurt her again.

Erdo walked over the hill as if nothing had happened. "I'm sorry I'm late. Did you need me?"

"I'm fine, thanks," said Maria. "I'll be going home now."

As she calmly and gratefully walked back to her car, she sensed that she was becoming a different person and had aged many years, perhaps many lifetimes, in those few moments. She had never felt so well, hopeful, and content.

"Well done, Amira," Erdo called out to Maria as he waved from the top of the hill.

Amira? thought Maria. *Erdo is old. Sometimes he gets his students' names muddled up.*

THE CALL TO LOVE

CHAPTER 11
NOBLE

Maria was turning twenty-one, and it had been more than four years since her accident. Her mother, Lucy, noticed she seemed to have aged years in the last few months.

"At twenty-one," Lucy said to her husband, "she knows more than you and I will ever know."

Most of Lucy's friends loved Maria. They still saw her as the sweet little girl given to Lucy and Lenny later in their marriage, who recovered from a terrible accident. They never bothered to look and see if Maria had grown up. Perhaps it was better that way.

Being a more recent friend, Verloren was different. She could see who Maria was. Maria was what Verloren was not. Verloren was nice to Maria whenever Lucy was present, but when Lucy stepped away, she dismissed her as if she were not worth noticing.

These days, Lucy often asked her daughter for advice.

One afternoon in the cafe, Lucy said, "Verloren was in tears today when she spoke about her marriage. She gets interested in other men. It never works out, and then she gets even more upset. I don't know what to say. Do you think you could help her?"

"I would love to help her," said Maria, "but she wouldn't listen to me. She might listen to you."

"What will I tell her?" asked Lucy.

"Tell her that her husband loves her as best as he can," said Maria. "And tell her not to look for other men. They won't be able to make her happy either."

"I can't tell her that," said Lucy. "She'll never speak to me again."

"It's the truth," laughed Maria. "She thinks she can make herself feel better by being chosen by someone she admires."

"Don't we all think that?" asked Lucy, without shame.

"Yes, Mamma," said Maria. "And it doesn't work for anyone."

ANOTHER EVENING, Lucy and Maria stood in their kitchen peeling vegetables for dinner.

"Why is Farkas so angry with us?" Lucy asked. "I don't mind that he doesn't come to our cafe anymore. I'm not offended. But when I see him on the street, he acts as if I asked him to leave. He won't even say hello. It makes me sad. I don't hold anything against anyone. He came to our cafe for a long time and..."

Lucy paused, searching for the right words, "...and I miss him."

"Don't worry," said Maria. "It's just him. In his mind, everyone has hurt him or will hurt him. He is protecting himself."

"Why would he think that?" asked Lucy. "He must have friends who love him. Everyone has friends."

"Do they?" said Maria. "Most have arrangements."

The conversation was getting too much for Lucy.

"Okay, darling," she said, "please get the hens' eggs and bring some lettuce back with you from the garden."

After dinner, Maria walked the few streets to Farkas's house and left some eggs at his front door with a note:

These are from Mum. She said she misses seeing you at the cafe.

Maria thought, *If Mum knew I said that, she would kill me.*
She laughed and ran home.

A few days later, Farkas came to get his morning coffee from Waldmeer Corner Store and Cafe. He ordered takeaway, told Lucy how good she looked, and then went outside to wait.

"I'll take it to him," Maria said when his name was called.

"Thank you," said Farkas as she handed him his coffee.

He hesitated. "I hate my name. I would like myself better if I had a better name."

"It's a beautiful name," said Maria. "It means *wolf*. Wolves don't like fighting, but are fierce when they need to be. Loyal. Intelligent. Sensitive. Noble. Why would you want to change that?"

CHAPTER 12
NO ONE CAN TAKE HER

In the Leleks:

Maria looked straight into Erdo's eyes and said, "I know who Amira is. I know why you called me that name last time I was here. She helped me with the nightmare. She talks to me all the time now."

"Yes," said Erdo. "Is that a problem?"

"Yes, it is," said Maria. "I hear Amira's voice so often, I think she is taking me over."

"And is *that* a problem?" asked Erdo.

"Yes," said Maria. "I want to get rid of her."

"I see," said Erdo without emotion.

"Amira is not from this world," said Maria. "She doesn't belong here. She will destroy my life. She doesn't give this life any value. I don't think she even wants to stay here. I won't be able to be a normal person. And I won't even be here much longer. She will take us both away."

"I see," said Erdo.

"I'm scared," said Maria.

"I can see that."

"I'm sorry. I know it's not what you want, but it's too much for me."

Erdo was not often sympathetic but said, "It's alright. No one is asking anything of you that you would not want for yourself. You are free. No one has to be a martyr. The powers that be are not interested in sacrifices."

Maria relaxed. "Oh, okay. Well, that is alright then."

"I have an idea," Erdo said enthusiastically. "Why don't you leave Amira here with me? She and I can have a good ol' catch-up, and she will wait for you in case you want her back."

"That sounds like a wonderful idea," said Maria. "I will leave her here with you."

She frowned slightly. "She will be safe, won't she? I wouldn't want anything to happen to her. No one will take her away?"

Erdo laughed.

"Trust me. No one can take her from me." He walked off as if he thought that was the most amusing thing he had heard in ages.

With delighted relief, Maria drove back to Waldmeer feeling like a normal person, a twenty-one-year-old girl, instead of a ten-thousand-and-twenty-one-year-old sage.

CHAPTER 13
ON MY OWN

It was true that Maria no longer had to deal with the challenges Amira brought into her life. However, she did not foresee that much of the life she loved had been created by Amira, not by her. Those parts of her life were already dismantling.

Without Amira, Maria was a kind, uncomplicated, and natural young woman, but nothing more. For all Farkas's resisting it, the thing that drew him to Maria was Amira. Amira could help him in a way that he could not help himself. She saw him as he truly was. On the other hand, Maria could only see what was before her eyes. Farkas had no need for a twenty-one-year-old girl in his life. He could run rings around her.

Maria hardly saw Farkas in town anymore. Sometimes, she walked past his house on the hill to see if there was any life there. It looked like no one was ever home, but she couldn't be sure. Maybe he had gone away. Perhaps he was sitting in his house, being a recluse. Maybe he was having a fabulous time doing all sorts of fun things. Wherever he was, he had made himself invisible to her.

As for Gabriel, he soon noticed the change in Maria. He didn't know why it happened, but he knew he felt bored around her. Too kind to tell her the truth, he casually mentioned one day that he had lots of work in the city. Charlie told Maria that Gabriel was busy with his city friends. Whatever he was busy with, it wasn't Waldmeer or Maria.

I guess Gabriel doesn't need the friendship of a young country girl who has only ever worked in the local cafe, Maria thought.

She would see him from the cafe window when he was in town on the odd occasion.

He didn't let me know he was here, she thought sadly.

Maria supposed it was a consolation that Elise and the other girls of Waldmeer also had lost interest in her. They no longer bothered to give her sideways glances, speak in hushed tones, or look straight past her as she passed them on the street. It seemed no longer necessary to undermine her.

Although a little puzzled by Maria's sudden character reversal, Lucy and Lenny had become used to the unexpected from Maria. They decided it was best to go with the flow. It was their saving grace in life.

Charlie still loved Maria, but these days she talked to her more like a little sister than an equal. Or perhaps it would be more accurate to say that Charlie previously treated Maria like a rarity found in an old op shop and treasured.

It was a revelation to Maria that even though people could find the Amira part of her uncomfortable, unpredictable, annoying, or illogical, it was also the part they had the most faith in. Their faith was not misplaced. Amira loved the most, forgave the most, understood the most, laughed the most, and had the most to give. Those who felt they had too much to lose from Amira's presence targeted her as an enemy. Now, both friends and enemies were gone.

Maria didn't blame anyone for losing interest in her; she even found herself somewhat lifeless and lost. She wasn't exactly unhappy with herself, but she felt she was a shadow of the person she had been.

She started walking on the beach after work, looking for something. The waves rolled in, one after the other, peaceful in their constancy. Maria needed silence. She got it.

CHAPTER 14
THE LONG BEACH

As Maria walked on the long beaches of Waldmeer, she often felt alone, both on and off the beach. It was not entirely true that she was alone because she still had Erdo, Charlie, her mother, and father.

Yet she *was* alone. No Amira. No Farkas. No Gabriel. She wondered why it would matter so much that Farkas and Gabriel were both gone. For quite a while, she hardly saw Farkas. When she did, his anger hovered just below the surface, ready to emerge if she did or said anything he felt warranted it. And Gabriel? Why did it matter that he didn't have time for Maria anymore? She had always known he had a full and busy life in the city.

Why does losing them feel like such a loss? thought Maria. *I didn't choose them to be in my life.*

They certainly would not have been obvious choices. One could be feral, and the other lived in a different world.

If I didn't choose them, maybe they chose me? she thought.

They would have as little chosen her as she would have chosen them.

Who made the choice, then? Maria wondered. *These choices seem to be made on their own. They bring as much sorrow as joy. Maybe more. Why? Are they designed to hurt us? Perhaps they bring hidden grace, but we struggle to find it.*

Maria looked at the seagulls powering low over the wild beach. Her mind was very still and quiet.

It is the light of love that connects us to others, she thought. *That is what we miss. The love. We answer the call of love. It comes from God and touches our souls.*

These were deep thoughts. Perhaps Amira was close by.

It is one thing to lose people you love, thought Maria. *It is another to lose yourself. That is a greater loss.*

"Life is not worth much to me without Amira," Maria called to the seagulls as they sat on the sand. "Even if I have no one else, I must, at least, have her."

The seagulls lifted in one communal effort and turned to sea.

She called after them, "I will get her back."

RETRIEVING AMIRA

CHAPTER 15
NORTH COUNTRY

In the Leleks:

"What do you mean she's not here?" said Maria. "You told me that no one would take her."

"Of course, no one took her," said Erdo. "She left of her own accord. She said she wanted to visit the North Country and see her friends in the Garden of Garourinn."

"But I want her back," said Maria.

"Calm down. You will have her back. My sister, Milyaket, is visiting me at the moment. She is the keeper of another forest. On her way home, she will happily take you to the North Country and you can retrieve Amira."

"My parents will worry if I am gone for long," said Maria.

"I will send a message to them saying you will be staying the week with Charlie," said Erdo. "That will be long enough."

I hope so, thought Maria.

"Thank you," she said. "It is quiet in the cafe, so my mother will be fine."

"Milyaket has all you need for the journey," said Erdo. "You will start immediately."

IN THE INTER-DIMENSIONAL NORTH COUNTRY:

Although Maria had never met Milyaket, she felt instantly familiar and comfortable.

She had much she wanted to ask Milyaket. In particular, she was curious about Erdo and Milyaket's family.

What sort of family is that? she wondered.

However, after a few words of introduction, Milyaket remained utterly silent and would not be drawn into any conversation. After numerous attempts, Maria accepted that the journey would be a silent one.

"When will we get there?" asked Maria.

"We will know," said Milyaket.

Strange answer, thought Maria.

Maria and Milyaket walked for several days. Milyaket had arranged for them to stay somewhere simple and safe each evening. Maria wondered who owned the little huts deep in the forest. As Milyaket was silent, Maria had no other place to go but into her thoughts.

As each hour passed, her thoughts became quieter and more organised. And as her thoughts became more tranquil, Maria noticed that the physical terrain changed somewhat.

Milyaket's silence had a hypnotising effect. It was rhythmic— steady and assured. It was a meditation in itself. Sometimes Maria forgot to think about what they were doing and where they were going. She didn't forget out of distraction or weariness. She felt acutely awake and alive.

By the third afternoon, the landscape had changed entirely, and they approached a mountain pass.

"We are here," said Milyaket. "We are entering the North Country. You will not need me from here. Go straight through the pass, and you will find the Garden of Garourinn on the other side. May the Great Ones be with you."

Maria would have been scared alone, except that her mind had become so quiet that fear seemed inappropriate. She tried to keep the same peaceful state of mind as she walked, but without Milyaket, it seemed much harder to do.

CHAPTER 16
PACK

I t was early evening, and Maria didn't seem to be getting any closer to the end of the pass. It was summer and relatively mild in the mountain air, but it seemed wise to get off the main path and find a sheltered spot for the night. Sitting in the fading light, she ate some of the food Milyaket had given her.

Suddenly, an uneasy stillness fell all around. The trees, the small animals, the wind, and even the plants held their breath as if waiting to see the outcome of an impending event. Maria looked around nervously, then gasped. A pack of about thirty wolves was circling her with eyes glued not to her meagre bits of food but to her.

I am the food, she thought.

Running would have been ridiculous. This pack was made of healthy, strong, vibrant creatures—masters of their terrain. Still terrified, an idea entered the tiny bit of quiet space that remained in her mind.

I love dogs. They are my friends. Wolves are ancient dogs. There is nothing to fear.

The largest wolf approached Maria and, to her surprise, she could understand him.

"You are Maria? My name is Galahad," said the wolf. "This is my pack. We guard the borders of Garourinn. We will keep you safe for the rest of your journey. We are travelling to the far border of Garourinn. Night is soon upon us. Come with us."

Not waiting for an answer, Galahad nodded for his pack to fall into line. The injured and elderly went first. This seemed a little mean to Maria, as they would be the most vulnerable to attack. However, she later found out that they set the pace. Some of the stronger males followed close behind them. Many of the females and young took their place in the centre ahead of the remaining male wolves. Some distance behind walked Galahad on his own.

A female wolf approached Maria and said, "My name is Sage. I am Galahad's mate. Walk with me."

It was almost dark, so they stopped at a cave for the night. A few of the hunters went out looking for nocturnal creatures. They soon came back with meat. Since her accident, Maria had been vegetarian. She couldn't eat cooked meat, let alone raw meat.

The wolves respected their prey's life and counted it as being as worthy as their own. They would accept their own death as they accepted the death of their prey. They did not place more importance on one life than on another. There was a sense that the Great Order of Life was to be trusted, that nothing could ever be taken from anyone that was rightfully theirs. Maria ate the last of the food she had.

The next day, Sage and the other bitches showed her where to find berries and various fruits. It looked like she would be with them some days. Each night, the pack stayed close, both for warmth and affection. Maria was happily included as if she belonged.

The invisible threads of togetherness were ever-present amongst the wolves. They were not possessive, controlling or needy. There was a simple order that everyone accepted for the pack's good. They found their happiness and stability in the well-being of all. Unlike humans, the wolves were instinctively oriented towards whatever made for a harmonious, well-functioning community.

Perhaps they are fortunate, Maria thought. *They do not struggle with choice. They simply are what they are.*

CHAPTER 17
BORDER

Galahad came from the back of the pack and took his stride beside Maria.

He must have something important to tell me, she thought.

"We will soon be at the entrance to the Garden of Garourinn," said Galahad. "We will leave you there as we cannot enter the garden. It is a privilege only for those who have the Spark of God in them."

"But you do have that spark," said Maria.

"It is our task to serve those with the spark," said Galahad. "In so doing, we may one day earn it ourselves. One of our ancestors sacrificed his life to save a baby human not far from here. He was badly wounded in a battle with a wolf from a foreign pack, but he managed to keep the child safe. He carried it to the border of Garourinn, where it was gratefully accepted. He did not know that it was the Head Gardener's youngest child. In return, our ancestor wolf was given the Spark of God. He died from his wounds but was then reborn as a human and began his long journey in a different dimension."

"That's beautiful," said Maria, "but he may have been better off staying as a wolf. You wolves are happy. Most humans are not."

"No," said Galahad. "It is a great honour to be human. Humans can freely choose their destiny. Farewell. It has been my happy duty to serve you."

"The honour has been all mine," said Maria with restrained emotion.

One doesn't crumble in front of an alpha wolf. They are too dignified. Each wolf came up, in turn, and rubbed its head on Maria's leg. Then, they turned as a pack and fell into place. She felt she would truly miss them and wished she could have a pack of wolves back home in Waldmeer, but that would hardly work.

MARIA HAD BEEN SITTING at the border of Garourinn for several hours. Not only did Amira not come, but no one else did either. She rested under a tree and drifted into a contented sleep. She could feel the filtered sun radiating from above. She dreamed that Amira was talking to her.

"Don't you think we have waited here long enough?" said Amira. "We have things to do back home."

It dawned on her that all her walking with Milyaket had called Amira back into her being. And her time with the wolves stabilised her presence even more. By the time they reached the border of Garourinn, Amira was reestablished within her.

In Waldmeer:

The following day, Maria woke in her bed.

"Nice to have you back again, darling," said Lucy, kissing her daughter. "We always miss you, even though you are only in the back hills. It has been quiet at the cafe, but we will be busy today. I will be glad of your help."

Maria could remember every detail of her trip to the North Country. Her travels were no longer disappearing into the ether.

CHAPTER 18
SEEING

Since Maria had retrieved Amira, they lived side by side more compatibly. Each would speak at a different time. Maria could now distinguish the two and choose which would get a voice. Previously, she had trouble even recognising who was who.

It was a satisfactory arrangement, although both knew that, in the end, one of them would prevail. Amira was stronger, but she would not step forward unless invited. Maria had to grow into her.

When Amira first entered Maria, she took on Maria's memories, longings, and hurts. Amira had to work with what she had inherited, and Maria had to learn to choose her freely.

The destination was sure. The timing was up to Maria.

GABRIEL WAS BACK. Maria asked him what he had been doing in the city.

"Not much," was the extent of Gabriel's reply.

He was back, but he was back in a different way. He was more directive. He sometimes got angry with Maria. It wasn't necessarily a bad thing. It meant that he trusted she would still be there.

Sometimes, when he wanted to put her in her place, he would say, "You are young. You have barely been away from Waldmeer. You have never even had a boyfriend. No offence, but there are lots of things you have no idea about."

To make sure that she got the point, he added, "And half the time, you live in a fantasy world. God only knows where."

Maria didn't mind. She had a power inside her. Who needs to quibble about details? She felt that Amira's temporary departure from her life was not the only cause of Gabriel's recent absence.

"Look," Gabriel said one afternoon, "I am a straightforward person. We all have friends. I have many. And you are entitled to be friends with whoever you want, but I don't like Farkas. I don't trust him. If you want to be friends with him, don't expect too much from me."

"I don't see Farkas anymore," said Maria.

Gabriel took no notice of her reply. It didn't seem to matter if she saw him or not. Maria tried to make light of the situation and made a joke. Gabriel didn't laugh.

She put her hand on his shoulder and said, "Everything is fine. Please don't worry about this."

Gabriel removed her hand.

She tried being firm and said, "This is silly."

Gabriel said, "I don't think so."

ON THE WALDMEER BEACH:

An advantage of having Amira back was that Maria found it was not as necessary to make the trip to the Leleks to see Erdo as often as she used to. She could tune into Amira. One evening, on the beach, she did just that about her recent conversation with Gabriel.

"This seems to me a no-win situation," said Maria. "I want Gabriel to be happy, but to make him happy, I have to accept his way of seeing life, which has problems. Besides, will it even make him happy? I doubt it."

"True," said Amira. "We all see a different reality and make decisions from that. Most believe that for one to gain, another must lose. Gabriel is guarding what he fears he could lose."

The sea was gentle. The waves were regular and soothing.

"A love that makes others lose will eventually turn on itself," continued Amira. "There is a deeper love that loves everyone. Know that—for yourself, for Gabriel, and for everyone."

HEALING

CHAPTER 19
DAUGHTER

"We are seeing you every weekend at the moment," Lucy said to Verloren.

"Yes, I have made an ongoing arrangement with Farkas," said Verloren.

Maria went still. A tightness formed in her stomach.

"I am doing a project with his garden," said Verloren, "and I will use it as a feature in one of our magazines. I come to Waldmeer every weekend now as there is a great deal to do, and I have huge plans."

"That's terrific for Farkas," said Lucy. "He gets free gardening. Who wouldn't want that?"

"Yes, it's a little more than that," said Verloren, almost sheepishly. "We are paying him considerably because otherwise, he wouldn't do it."

"It's all worth it," she added brightly, "because I want that particular garden, and the result will be stunning."

The tightness in Maria's stomach deepened.

That evening, at dinner, Lucy told her husband about Verloren's project in Farkas's garden.

"Yeah, I already know," said Lenny. "Farkas's neighbour told me. I don't get it. Who would pay to work in someone else's garden? Does she fancy him or somethin'?"

"Lenny!" scolded Lucy. "Of course not. People like Verloren don't 'fancy' people. They are all class."

IT ONLY TOOK a few months for Verloren and Farkas to establish a pattern that would remain constant throughout their relationship. Verloren knew Farkas did not respect her. She wanted respect. More than that, she wanted love.

It would have been easier if the pain had been constant. But it wasn't. There were moments of light. A soft word. A glance. Enough to make her believe it might one day become something more.

She guarded the relationship jealously. If Maria's name was mentioned, she dismissed it as dull, as if she were nothing.

Maria felt it was not good for Farkas to have Verloren so close, no matter the money. He believed he was in control. He wasn't. It was the opposite of a healing relationship.

ONE DAY IN THE CAFE, Verloren walked past Maria briskly, and the cups went flying. Verloren didn't apologise or even seem to notice.

Lucy stiffened.

"Are you alright, Maria?" she asked.

Verloren turned quickly. "Oh, I'm sure she's fine. She is much tougher than she looks."

Her voice softened. "Poor little Maria. You have had enough challenges, haven't you, dear girl? Why, only the other day, someone said to me, 'Maria has had such a marvellous recovery from her accident, although she has been quite different since the accident. Her parents must wonder if it's even the same person!'"

No one said that to Verloren. It came. And she used it.

Lucy smiled weakly. "Yes, we are lucky."

She did not feel lucky.

Verloren's words felt like water slipping through the cracks.

Lucy kept hearing them.

"Her parents must wonder if it's even the same person."

There was a little too much truth in it. It was not a truth Lucy could handle.

CHAPTER 20
THE SHRINE

In the back hills:

The unstated yet unmistakable shift in Maria's relationship with her mother gave her the idea to move out. It was a good step, and both spoke positively about it without naming the real reason. Maria moved quietly on the arranged day and began living with Charlie, who was thrilled to have her. Charlie had a shed that was occasionally used for visitors, and it was now Maria's home.

Charlie's house was small and, like most artists', cluttered, which made it seem even smaller. It had her bedroom, a bedroom for Gabriel when he was there, and a room that had become the art studio. Gabriel used an old machinery shed for his sculpting studio. That way, he didn't have to spend too long in the house with Charlie.

For cheaper rent, Maria looked after the garden and the animals. She couldn't have been happier with the arrangement and was in her element. The shed was small but, when she shut the door, it belonged only to her.

It had a bed, a small kitchen, and an outside toilet that she shared with the spiders. She used the main house for a shower. Maria loved everything about it. She wanted her tiny home to be a healing space. Gabriel called it *Maria's Shed*, but Charlie called it *Maria's Shrine* because of the candles, the holy pictures, and how it felt.

Charlie often found reasons to come to the Shrine. She said it felt so nice. A relief from the clutter in her house and in her mind. Gabriel occasionally came to the door, but he had never been inside. He behaved as though there were an invisible barrier at the entrance. While Charlie walked straight through it, he could not, or would not.

SOME MONTHS LATER, Charlie was swearing at the chooks. And the dogs. And anything that moved. Her girlfriend of the past year, Elizabeth, had cheated on her and had confessed a few days earlier.

"She is having one of her attacks," Gabriel said quietly to Maria, rolling his eyes. "I have to go back to the city now. I will leave you with the crazy woman."

Maria waved goodbye as he drove his car down the long dirt track to the front gate.

These days, she missed him when he returned to the city.

"Come on, Charlie," she said, trying to break the tension. "It's been three days. You're still acting like a lunatic."

"You bet I am," said Charlie, with more expletives than ordinary words. "That daughter of a bitch cheated on me."

"I'll make you a cup of tea," Maria said, taking her hand and leading her into the Shrine.

Charlie had not visited the Shrine for a few days, which was unusual for her. She felt she couldn't go in there and swear and fume without feeling ashamed. So she stayed away. She was too angry.

Maria spoke softly, gave her tea, lit some candles, and let her talk. She talked for an hour without stopping. Maria listened.

Gradually, Charlie's voice became less loud, less furious. Then she began to cry. Soon she was howling. Maria let her cry without touching her. She did not want to interrupt the process.

"I know you'll tell me not to," Charlie said at last, "because you're such a goodie-two-shoes, but I hate Elizabeth. I can't help it. I hate her."

"No, you don't," Maria said. "You love her. You're hurt."

When Charlie had had enough and was ready to go back to her own house, Maria walked her to the door.

"Trust that you will be okay," she said. "You will be. Talk to Elizabeth without the hate. Listen to what she says. See what's still there between you. If it can be mended, mend it. If not, let her go."

Charlie stood quietly for a moment, then nodded.

"You loved her once," Maria said. "She is still that person, whether you are together or not."

CHAPTER 21
GENTLE CORRECTOR

Maria didn't walk on the beaches as often now. After work she had to drive to the back hills to get home. However, the beach was the place—vast, changing, and unchanging—where she heard Amira's voice most clearly. Today she was walking and listening.

"You sense that Farkas means you no harm and that Verloren does," said Amira. "So you are willing to send goodwill to Farkas but not Verloren."

Amira was a gentle but direct corrector.

"At this point," Amira continued, "that is unacceptable."

Maria wondered who it was "unacceptable" to and what "point" she was at.

"I see," said Maria, who was not sure she saw at all.

"Every ugly drama can become a blessing if you see it differently," said Amira. "No one suffers on purpose. Healing comes when we see differently. The question is: do you want suffering or peace? It's that simple."

"Hmm," said Maria. "That's a fairly obvious choice, but let me think about it some more!"

"As you wish," said the ever-patient Amira. "Remember, when you see differently, you are choosing to sit where it is sunny and warm."

LUCY HAD NOT SPOKEN to Lenny about Maria leaving home or about Verloren's comments that she was a different person since the accident. Both were too raw, and she didn't want to give them more power than they already had.

This evening, it was time.

"Maria decided to walk on the beach after work today," Lucy told her husband.

"How is she going?" asked Lenny.

"She loves living at Charlie's," said Lucy.

"That's good," said Lenny. "We want her to be happy."

The thought of Maria's happiness opened the door for Lucy.

"Verloren said that people wonder if Maria is the same person since the accident," she said. "What if she isn't our daughter?"

She felt silly saying it, but it felt worse to leave it unsaid.

Lenny stopped reading the paper, looked up at the woman he had married when he was seventeen, and said, "If we have a daughter with the angels and also a daughter who lives near us, works happily with you every day, and loves us both, then we are very fortunate. We would have *two* daughters, Lucy, not *none*."

Lucy looked at her husband of thirty-five years. She felt very blessed about everything.

THE FOLLOWING weekend Maria overheard her mother say to Verloren as she left the cafe, "My daughter decided she is too old to live at home anymore, but daughters never really leave their mothers."

Verloren stopped walking and looked at Lucy, whose voice was even and forgiving. She didn't hold anything against Verloren. She saw the whole thing as an opportunity for growth and felt quietly pleased with her small victory over herself.

"She will always be my daughter," said Lucy, "no matter where she lives. I will always love her, and it is love that makes her my daughter."

BODY

CHAPTER 22
FEAR

Charlie and Maria were headed for the Post Office in Waldmeer one lovely, sunny morning. Their sunny mood was interrupted by a lone male voice and snickering.

"You still kissin' girls, Charmaine?" said the man-boy.

The intention was to insult. However, Charlie felt it was more insulting to be called Charmaine than to have anyone comment on who she was kissing.

"Those idiot boys," she groaned.

Maria knew them well. It was a group of boys from her school year level. She didn't like them then. She still didn't.

Bullies, she thought, *led by the biggest bully of all, Harry Maclary.*

Harry's parents owned the dairy outside Waldmeer. He was spoiled, not so much with material things, but with too much pandering and too little responsibility. The result was not pleasant. At school, Harry and his hoon mates often tormented Maria.

You still a virgin? they would say to her loudly. *We can help you with that.*

They would then laugh and amble off proudly. Maria was

quiet at school and found them embarrassing, offensive, and scary.

Harry was pleased with the annoyed look on Charlie's face and said, "Or you kissin' that pussy-boy you live with?"

The boys found this even funnier. Charlie was no pushover. She had a mouth on her and a spirit to match. However, to Maria's surprise, she withdrew instead of firing up. She remembered that Charlie had recently had more upsetting confrontations with her girlfriend, Elizabeth, and she must have felt defeated.

Harry opened his big mouth again, now that he was on a roll. The other boys looked on with amusement, as if it were the best morning fun they'd had in a while.

Suddenly, Maria swung around and headed straight for Harry. She disregarded the other boys, who instinctively moved out of the way. Maria had her eyes tunnelling into Harry. He looked startled and tried to regain his position. Every memory of his abusive, threatening behaviour towards her and every other vulnerable girl he had harassed came to the forefront of her mind. His current remarks about Charlie and Gabriel only added fuel to the fire.

Looking for support, Harry nodded to his boys, who circled Maria and stood a foot above her. Charlie disappeared from view as the tower of boys closed in. Maria was not afraid—not anymore.

She thought, *You can hurt my body, but I don't care. I will never allow you to hurt my soul ever again. And you will not hurt those I love.*

Maria poked a finger into Harry's chest and said, "Do not come into our cafe, Harry Maclary, until you have learned some manners."

Did she say *Harry Maclary*? She might have said *buffoon*. Either way, he got the point. Harry was so shocked that quiet little Maria had lost her fear that he stood there dumbly, and the boys decided to open a path for her to let her out.

When Charlie and Maria got around the corner, they

collapsed into laughter. It all seemed so ridiculous, including Maria's reaction.

~

IN THE BACK hills of Waldmeer:

Maria drove up the long driveway to her little shed the following Saturday after work. Gabriel was back for the weekend. He walked up to her car and smiled.

"Charlie told me about your run-in with the buffoon," he said. "Thank you for defending my 'pussy-boy' status, but you don't need to bother. I am fine."

"Of course you are fine," said Maria.

"Well, don't put yourself in that position next time," said Gabriel protectively.

~

IN WALDMEER:

A few days later, while visiting the cafe, Charlie decided to tell Lucy about the incident with the hoon-boys while Maria was out getting fruit and vegetables. Charlie was like that. *Why hide things?* she thought.

That evening Lucy, in turn, told Lenny. Lucy was a mother. She tended to be understanding of the problems of other people's children. She would say, "There, but for the grace of God, go I," and be thankful that, somehow, she had cornered lots of God's grace.

Lenny said nothing, but he was a father. His job was to protect. Harry and those boys had better watch out the next time they crossed paths with the longtime fisherman of Waldmeer.

~

A SMALL POSY of flowers was delivered to Waldmeer Corner Store and Cafe a few weeks later, with Maria's name on it. There was no sender's name. It was the sort of posy with pretty pink paper you buy if you don't have much money but want to impress someone.

It had a little handwritten note by someone who looked as though they were trying to write neatly but didn't write very often.

Sorry, Maria, that's all it said.

The writing looked familiar.

A memory from school arose.

Maria smiled.

She had already forgiven Harry.

After all, forgiveness is something you give *yourself.*

CHAPTER 23
VASTANDAMINE FOREST

I n the back hills of Waldmeer:
One night, around two in the morning, Maria woke in her tiny shed home. The night sky was perfectly clear, filled with brilliant stars. Someone was standing beside her bed. Maria was relieved to see that it was Milyaket.

She smiled at Maria and said, "It's lovely seeing you again. How did you go crossing the North Country pass after I left you?"

Maria felt that Milyaket already knew exactly what had happened, but, to be polite, she said, "Well, I met the wolf pack, and Galahad took me to the border of Garourinn, and there I realised Amira had already returned to me."

"That's wonderful," said Milyaket. "Now I have somewhere else to take you. Someone is waiting to see you in the Vastandamine Forest in the Homeland."

The Vastandamine Forest was where Farkas had met his Earth father.

"If you think so," Maria said hesitantly.

She wondered who would be waiting there for her.

IN THE INTER-DIMENSIONAL HOMELAND:

Milyaket took her hand, and before any time seemed to pass, Maria was sitting in the forest in full daylight on a grassy patch beside one of the happy rivers dancing along its way. After a few minutes, a man appeared and sat next to her.

"Zufar," said Maria as she hugged and kissed him.

Maria didn't know who Zufar was. Amira certainly did, although it had been eons since she had seen him.

LIFETIMES AGO:

Zufar and Amira were lifelong mates. They fell in love as young adults and were soon married. It was a good, spirited match, and they gave much to each other. Many of their joint life lessons came from their bodies. Sometimes people love each other and connect in their minds or hearts but never really connect in their bodies. Zufar was a soldier and strongly aligned with his healthy body. He was also very aligned with Amira's body. They were as much at home with each other's bodies as they were with their own.

In those days, soldiers spent long periods overseas, and many slept with other women while away. Although Zufar did not do this for several years, eventually he did. Amira knew as soon as he returned. His body was different. Part of it felt foreign. Both decided it was best not to talk about it. They tried to focus on the essence of their love rather than the betrayals to it. They worked to get the purity of their connection back. It took time, but they did get it back. That is, until the next long trip away.

As time passed, Zufar learned to control his sexual drive rather than let it control him. It was a happy day when next he returned home. His body felt as it did when he left home. However, as Zufar learned to transcend his body's desires, he also began to transcend the idea of separate and conflicting bodies altogether. He found that he could no longer kill another person. He could not see anyone as an enemy anymore. This was an outstanding achievement as a soul, but a serious conflict as a soldier now in command.

One time he confronted an enemy to protect one of his men. The soldier escaped. Zufar was unable to harm the enemy and was killed instead. As his guides took him to the Homeland, he told them he was pleased to be going home and no longer wished to live in a world where brothers were seen as enemies. He knew he would see Amira again.

Amira was the one left behind. The grief forced her to learn that souls can never be separated. She could see that even though we have a body that can thrive and be used for beautiful things, it is the changeless soul that connects. After that she often felt Zufar near her and sometimes even heard his voice. Her grief was completely healed. Further, the very capacity for grief was dismantling.

In the Homeland:

"It has been a long time," said Zufar.

Amira nodded.

"I have come to tell you," continued Zufar, "that I will soon be travelling to a different dimension, and you will not feel me around for a long time. It is my happy duty to go, but I wanted to let you know."

"My dear, you are so kind to bring me here to say goodbye," said Amira, taking Zufar's hand. "We have already said more goodbyes than are necessary. Those were goodbyes that brought about the end of partings. You have your work, which will bring you great fulfilment, and I have mine. We taught each other that no parting is possible."

Zufar stood and looked beyond the trees to a distant land.

He turned to Amira, knelt before her, and said, "Then there shall be no parting."

He rose, walked towards the trees, and disappeared.

Maria had been totally voiceless while witnessing Zufar and Amira. She did not know what to say.

"Come," said Amira. "We have work to do and people who need us. It is time to go."

~

In the back hills of Waldmeer:

The stars were no longer shining through Maria's window. The sun was creeping over the hill. The hens were making a racket, and the morning was calling. It was the beginning of a clear and glorious day.

CHAPTER 24
A BETTER BOOK

In Waldmeer:

One afternoon, Harry Maclary's twin sister, Mary, entered the cafe. Mary was the opposite of Harry. Reserved, clever, peaceful, polite—an altogether delightful young woman. By now, all three—Harry, Mary, and Maria—were twenty-three.

"I'm so sorry about my brother," said Mary. "You know what he can be like."

She added hopefully, "I'm sure with a few more years he will work himself out."

"Of course, he will," said Maria, smiling to let Mary know not to give the incident any more thought.

Mary turned to leave but hesitated and quietly said, "Umm, I was wondering if you had a minute?"

"Yes, of course," said Maria.

"I have a problem," said Mary. "And I can't talk to my family about it or anyone else in Waldmeer. They are so conservative."

"Yes," said Maria encouragingly.

"I realised some time ago that I am not attracted to boys," said Mary. "Last time I went to the city, I met a gay girl there, and it dawned on me that I am also gay. There is no one here in Wald-meer that I am interested in. I mean, are there even any gay people in our little town? I just wanted to tell someone who would not repeat what I have said."

Maria smiled and said, "I don't think that's a problem at all. Relationships are valuable no matter who they are between."

Mary looked relieved.

"I think you must come and have dinner at my house," Maria said.

"I'd love to," replied Mary.

"Then come tonight after I finish work," said Maria. "Charlie's property is beautiful, and it will still be light enough for us to walk along Merri Creek."

CHARLIE INSTANTLY LIKED Mary and felt relaxed around her. So relaxed that she soon delved into a deep and honest conversation about Elizabeth. She complained about her girlfriend's numerous infidelities and the almost totally collapsed state of their relation-ship. Maria let Mary and Charlie do the talking.

"I don't think we have to stay in a repeating bad story," said Mary with calm maturity. "We can pick up a new book that is better and happier just by putting the other book down."

Maria smiled. It was as she thought. Mary was a good match for Charlie, and vice versa. Charlie's life and career were thriving at thirty-five, and she no longer needed to look to other people to make her way. At this stage it would not matter to her that Mary was younger and only starting her adult life.

In the past, Charlie had always been drawn to women like herself, full of fire. She enjoyed the energy, power, and life force of those relationships. They helped her become who she now was, but they were also full of damaging fireworks. Fire doesn't need more fire. It needs water—calm, healing, restorative water. That was Mary. She was mostly *water*, a substantial bit *earth* for practicality and stability, and a little *air*. Without a little *air*, Mary would not have been able to relate to the creative in Charlie or herself.

Maybe it's a match made in Heaven, thought Maria, *but maybe not.*

Relationships are a gift from God. One cannot arrange what is not written in Heaven. Both people must feel the spark of God, which ignites the love and says, "Come this way. I have a good story for you."

BEING SAVED

CHAPTER 25
VISITOR

In Waldmeer:

"I'm going to sell my house," Farkas said to Verloren, who was in Waldmeer for the weekend working on her gardening project.

"What?" said a shocked Verloren. "No, I like coming here."

"Then you can buy it," said Farkas.

Verloren liked coming when Farkas was in the house, not when he wasn't. He had already made up his mind about selling, and Verloren did end up buying it. She and her husband would use it as a holiday house.

Farkas knew he needed to go somewhere away from Waldmeer. He didn't know where. However, someone else did know.

∼

In the back hills of Waldmeer:

Maria had just returned from work and settled into her comfy chair. Charlie didn't bother knocking.

"Come and see who came out of the forest today," Charlie said excitedly.

"Is it Erdo?" Maria asked. She hadn't seen him for quite a while and would love to.

"It's not a *he*," said Charlie, enjoying the suspense. She pointed to her back door.

"She was ravenous and had a leg injury," said Charlie. "I don't know how long she has been wandering around the forest."

There, on the mat, lay a dog. She was obviously tired, but got on her feet as Maria approached.

"Isn't she a beautiful German shepherd?" said Charlie. "A few days' rest and food and she will be magnificent."

Maria stopped walking.

"That's not a German shepherd," she said. "It's a wolf."

"Don't be ridiculous," said Charlie. "We don't have wolves in our forest."

Maria and Charlie shared many things, but some things Maria kept to herself. It was not only a wolf but Sage, Galahad's mate, from the North Country. Maria could see from Sage's eyes that she recognised her. Perhaps, Sage even came to find her.

She followed Maria back to her shed and, much to Charlie's disappointment, would not leave Maria's side again.

In Waldmeer:

Sage refused to be left at home in the mornings and travelled with Maria to Waldmeer Corner Store and Cafe each day. Maria had the uneasy feeling that keeping a wolf as a domestic pet was doomed to fail, but she was so thrilled to have her that she would not allow herself to think about it.

"You stay in the back area," she said to Sage as she headed back into the cafe.

Sage would sit obediently, but sometimes Maria would check on her and she would be gone. The fences were high. It was a mighty jump, but Sage was used to the wild country up north, and a fence would certainly be no problem.

Sage seemed to be scouting for something. When she couldn't find it, she would return to the cafe and try again later. She was agile and adept at keeping a low profile so that no one seemed to notice that there was a wolf in their midst.

One day Sage was gone longer than usual, and Maria started to worry. Eventually she returned, but she looked different. She pulled on Maria's hand, urging her to open the gate and follow. She seemed to have found what she was looking for.

She took Maria past her parents' house and stopped outside Farkas's. Maria's heart sank.

Sage looked calmly into her eyes.

"All right, girl," said Maria, "do as you must."

Farkas was in the process of his final packing, as the Reisendens were taking possession of the house the next day. His door was open.

Sage went inside with one last backward glance at Maria.

The door closed after her, and Maria slowly walked back down the hill.

She didn't come for me, sighed Maria. *She came for Farkas. He needs her more than me.*

CHAPTER 26
CLOUDS

Farkas recognised Sage immediately. Not only that, but he found he could speak with her as fluently as with a human, probably more so. They headed for the Leleks, crossed Erdo's walking bridge, and began the long walk to the North Country.

Farkas had never been on the bridge before. He hesitated a moment, but Sage nudged him on.

He now knew where he had to go—back to the pack.

He remembered much in the next few weeks of travelling with Sage.

"It will be winter soon in the North Country," he said.

"You will be alright," said Sage. "You can use the abandoned hut. Galahad will get enough supplies for you from the Garden of Garourinn to last the winter. You will remember how to live there once we arrive. We will help you."

IN THE INTER-DIMENSIONAL NORTH COUNTRY:

After a short period of adjustment, Farkas settled into life in the North Country. For the first time in as long as he could remember, he began to feel genuinely happy and relaxed.

He loved the companionship of the wolf pack and the rhythm of daily life. The harsh conditions did not bother him at all. He had fire, water, and food. The pack would often bring him the kill so he could take what he wanted first. He *did* cook it.

He could recall much about life in the pack, although he had been a human for a long time. Sometimes, he let the pack stay in the hut overnight, but that was rare.

He played with them often and laughed a lot. He found them very funny. They took great pleasure in amusing him, and the play was very healing for Farkas.

One day, close to the end of winter, Farkas went for a long walk over an adjoining mountain. He had not seen the pack that day, which was unusual.

After a few hours of walking in soothing, relatively warm sunlight, Farkas began to feel hungry. So he turned for home.

Only then did he notice the mass of dark clouds approaching quickly across the sky.

It was not good.

Once they reached him it would be freezing cold, and he would barely be able to see anything. He would have to trust his internal compass to find his way back to the hut.

After half an hour he was surrounded by cold, swirling darkness and had lost his bearings. He did not know which direction to walk, and he was still several hours from the hut.

Worse, his mind began dissolving into a sea of disturbing images that grew more intense with every passing minute.

Everywhere he looked in the moving darkness were images of past hurts—people he felt had betrayed him—and a mass of sorrows and anger in every imaginable form.

It was relentless.

Who would think that we could hold so many grievances?

Many of the people he could not even recognise. Yet they contributed to the throbbing grey beast now hunting him from every angle.

Farkas found a ledge and sat beneath it, trying to shield himself from the bitter wind. He wouldn't survive long if he stayed there, but he did not want to go back into the tormenting gloom.

He could neither defeat it nor even understand it.

The image of a man appeared to his right.

Farkas assumed it was another of the tormenting images and pressed himself closer to the rock face. He tried to dismiss it, but it would not move.

"I see you have returned," said the stranger.

The other images had been voiceless. This one spoke.

"We have met before," the man continued. "You once saved my youngest child and paid for it with your own life. I gave you a different life—a human one."

Now Farkas knew who it was.

It was the Head Gardener from the Garden of Garourinn.

He jumped to his feet in relief and respect.

"We will walk together. You are not alone, but you must do as I ask," said the Head Gardener, who had already turned into the multitude of gruelling images.

"I don't want to go back out there," said Farkas.

"It is the only way for you to get back home," said the Head Gardener. "All these images are of your own making. You created them, and your anger feeds them and keeps them alive. You have given them all the power they possess. Walk through them, and they will dissolve. I cannot do that for you, but I can show you which direction to walk. You must do the walking yourself. Let us go, or it will be night before we reach the end of them."

Farkas did as the Head Gardener asked. He only half believed it would work.

Yet as he looked directly at each image and walked through it, it disintegrated.

Each one was quickly replaced by another harrowing vision. But as he continued walking, he grew more confident in the process.

He sensed he was making progress.

A faint glimmer of light appeared in the darkness.

Eventually the great mass of images began to thin.

Relieved and exhausted, he could see his home mountain in the distance.

A small moving blur was heading down from the mountain toward him.

It was the pack.

"I must return to the Garden now," said the Head Gardener. "Remember this, Farkas. Every grievance you hold hides a little more of the world's light from your eyes until the darkness becomes overwhelming. Everything you forgive restores that light. So ask yourself—who is it that you are really hurting?"

CHAPTER 27
SPECIAL

I n Waldmeer:

It was a sad time for Verloren. Farkas's house had a quick settlement, and she was soon unlocking the door with her own key instead of knocking and waiting for Farkas to open it for her. Despite his ambivalence towards her and sometimes abuse, Verloren would miss him greatly in the coming months.

It was a childish and irrational wish to want Farkas to love her —but don't we all do this?

We make people special to us, believing they can save us. Verloren was perhaps more obvious in her quest, less reserved than others, and more aggressive in what she wanted. But who could blame her for doing something we nearly all do, even if others do it with more grace? It is still the same idea: that someone else can save us from ourselves.

With time, Verloren would probably transfer that longing to another person, with a version of the same results. Don't we do that too? When one thing doesn't work, we look elsewhere to be saved. We rarely question the concept itself.

Sometimes, we don't look to another person to save us, but to money, acknowledgement, a title, a cause, or a notion of ourselves. None of it can save us. We travel the path differently; some are more polite, some are ruthless, some are clever, and some are instinctive. In the end, it all leads to the same despairing place.

Amid all this searching and not finding, Verloren was given a special gift. She now had a house in Waldmeer that carried a healing energy capable of helping people—if they would let it. In the quiet, unsuspecting moments, there it was. It brought a sense of peace and a feeling that everything was fine without searching for anything to be saved by. It softened the grasping for love and the blaming that followed when that grasping failed.

One evening, while walking back to her newly acquired house in the fading light, Verloren remembered a dream she once had. In the dream, her grandfather had told her how to reach the Garden of Garourinn. A person called the Head Gardener had suggested she revisit it in her sleep.

She had the dream a long time ago. In all that time, Verloren had not thought about it even once.

That night, as she lay her head on the pillow and drifted off to sleep while listening to the faint waves in the distance, a thought crossed her mind.

I might be able to find the Garden of Garourinn in my dreams.

She was, at last, looking in a place that could actually help her.

NEW BEGINNING

CHAPTER 28
MOVING

I *n the back hills of Waldmeer:*
　　One weekend in late winter, everyone sat on Charlie's veranda listening to the early evening sounds—and to Gabriel's idea. His living arrangement in the city had changed, and he had found a large, rambling house in one of the alternative inner-city suburbs. He proposed that everyone move there—he, Maria, Charlie, and Mary.

"It has three big bedrooms," said Gabriel. "One for me, one for Maria, and one for Charlie and Mary."

Since Mary first visited Charlie's property, she and Charlie had become inseparable. Elizabeth was long gone. Mary had an excellent effect on Charlie, who now had a calmness that had been absent before, adding to her already successful direction.

"Mary wants to start her university studies," Gabriel continued, "and Charlie has so many offers in the city that she could spend all week responding to them. The house has a workshop at the back, which Charlie and I can share, and a shop front which we can use as a gallery. There is a closed-in side veranda which I think Maria should use. She could start to see people and help them."

"How?" asked Maria.

"I don't know," said Gabriel, frustrated by the question. "How would I know? You will work it out once we get there. Turn it into a *Shrine*. You know how much Charlie loves going into your *Shrine* here. If she likes it, other people will too."

He said it as if only people like Charlie would want to go into it, not people like him. Yet, he was the one who thought up the idea, so he could not have been that dissociated from it.

Everyone just nodded, and that was that. They were moving.

Charlie went to the local Waldmeer real estate and told them she would rent out her property. The rent would pay the mortgage for now. That way she wasn't completely cutting her ties with Waldmeer.

CHAPTER 29
CANDLES

Maria closed the door of her shed one last time. There was no lock on it. There had never been.

She realised she had left two pictures and several half-used candles on the windowsill. For some reason, she decided to leave them there, although she had been told to empty the shed completely for the future renters.

"Goodbye, my dear home," she said to the Shrine. "You have loved me, so I leave part of myself here with you."

BY EARLY SPRING, Farkas was back in Waldmeer.

There was not much to rent, so he took Charlie's property. The isolated location suited him after the North Country mountains. To help with the rent, he decided to rent out Maria's old shed.

However, each time he called into the real estate agent to let them know, he would get to the desk, make some excuse, and walk out again.

I'll do it another day, he kept telling himself.

One morning after a storm, Farkas noticed the shed door had blown open. When he went to close it, he saw something on the windowsill.

Maria has left some of her stuff behind, he thought.

He sat on the bare floor and listened. Not for anything in particular. It was calm and still after the storm.

He got up, lit one of the candles, and sat down again.

It's Maria, Farkas said to himself. *I can feel Maria is here. It must be that candle. She always was a strange girl.*

It was Amira more than Maria, but Farkas could not distinguish them. Nor did he even know Amira's name. He only knew Maria, who was now gone.

Farkas sat there a long time. He didn't move.

"I'm sorry," he eventually said.

Farkas was not a man who said sorry. There would have been too much to say sorry for.

You did well, said the candle.

It sounded like Maria's voice, but older. More distant, yet also very close.

"You were brave to come anywhere near me," said the voice. "At some level, you knew that every thought you cherished would be taken apart, every grudge you harboured would be thrown back at you, and every ancient dream you held would be put into the fire."

Farkas didn't say anything. He was a little pleased that he could hear the voice. He knew it was a gift, but also an earned right.

"It is not just desperation that does that," continued the voice. "It is a belief in oneself—that one can do better, that one is worth it."

After a bit, Farkas got up and blew the candle out.

If he wanted to speak to Maria again, she might come back if he lit one of the half-used candles. He wanted to save them.

Opening the door of the little shed, he smelled the sweet freshness after the storm.

Maria's words went with him as he walked out into the day.

You did well.

PART II
IN ERALDUS

THE DIVIDING LINE

THE CITY

CHAPTER 30
MONEY

In Eraldus:

Gabriel sat down on Maria's bed as he had done many times in the city house, which they were now sharing with Charlie and Mary in Eraldus.

"I know you are trying your best, but you need to earn more money," said Gabriel. "Our first six-month lease is up, and they are increasing our rent."

As suggested back in Waldmeer, Maria set up the veranda as a healing space. It wasn't lacking clients. Most days, people knocked on the house door asking for the healing girl. She listened to their problems and helped them as much as she could.

"You have lots of clients, and they love you," said Gabriel. "You should be making lots of money by now."

He paused and thought he sounded too materialistic.

"I just don't understand it. That's all. I never see you buying anything for yourself. Where does your money go?"

Maria had not explained to him that her spirit counterpart, Amira, had told her that she was not to charge any money for healing. She was allowed to have a donation box. Many of the people who came had less money than Maria or had children and more urgent needs. She didn't want to take their money. Those who had money didn't necessarily give it. Generally, those with no money insisted on giving the most. Maria felt that what was freely given to her by the spirit world must be freely shared with others, although that was not right for everyone. Otherwise, no one would be making any money.

Without mentioning Amira, Maria explained the donation box to Gabriel. She already knew what the response would be.

"Please don't worry about me. I have enough for our rent and bills, and I am fine," she said.

Later that evening, Maria told Charlie what Gabriel had been saying to her.

"He said not to tell you," said Charlie, "but you haven't been paying your full share of the rent for the past six months. He has been adding to your share to make it equal to ours. He said it would give you a chance to get on your feet financially. Otherwise, the rent would be too much for you. Now, the rent is going up, and he thinks you still aren't able to pay the first amount, let alone the new amount."

"Oh, I see," said Maria.

It is one thing to make choices about one's lifestyle and quite another to be a burden on someone else.

It isn't just the money, thought Gabriel as he worked on one of his sculpture projects in the workshop. *Maria has become quite spacey and ungrounded since living in the city.*

He didn't know if it was the effect of all the troubled people she was seeing, if it was living in the city that didn't agree with her, or if it was living with him, Charlie, and Mary. He felt that putting her mind to the practical task of making money would bring her back into a more functional space.

The next day, he overheard the manager at their local cafe say she was looking for staff. He told her about Maria's experience in her mother's cafe in Waldmeer. The manager already knew Maria from coming to the cafe, and she liked her from day one. She liked all the residents of their house.

"Of course, we'll take her. She can have a shift tomorrow as someone is sick," said the manager.

"Thank you for finding me a proper job," Maria said to Gabriel somewhat apologetically. "I will start tomorrow."

The issue seemed resolved, and both put the minor upset out of their minds. Little did they realise it was the forerunner of a real fight.

CHAPTER 31
SEEING SOULS

Maria would often see the souls of people around her. Some were faint, others obvious, and some transparently clear. She had to remind herself that most people could not see what she saw and therefore did not have the same information.

She did not see souls exactly with her eyes, although there could sometimes be visual elements. It was more a knowing. A subtle transfer of understanding about the person's inner state, the stage of their soul's development, and the issues they were working through.

If someone had a life-threatening illness or a serious accident, Maria would sometimes know whether it was their time to pass on. If someone had suicidal thoughts, she could often sense how serious the situation was.

She could also feel the presence of those who had recently died near the people they loved. Dead mothers, in particular, seemed drawn to her. Of course, no one is truly dead, and that was the irony.

Maria had little, if any, control over what she did or did not see.

Six months after her accident as a teenager, she had an experience that taught her an invaluable lesson.

One of her great-aunts was very ill, and those around her knew death was near. The great-aunt's sister asked Maria to visit the dying woman, but Maria did not go.

Not long after the funeral, the great-aunt confronted her.

"You didn't go and say goodbye to her," she said. "And now it's too late."

Maria was surprised. "Aunty, why are you angry with me?"

"You should have gone to see her," the woman said.

Still confused, Maria replied, "But none of it matters now."

She meant that it would not matter to the deceased great-aunt. Now that she had passed, she would understand how unbreakable the ties of love are, and that no one had truly gone anywhere.

Understandably, her great-aunt did not appreciate Maria's response. She looked at her as if she must be terribly mean.

What a mismatch of communication lines.

After that, Maria always reminded herself that most people believed the dead had gone away, perhaps even ceased to exist entirely. She had to be careful not to say things that sounded cruel when she was simply unconcerned because, from her perspective, there was nothing to be concerned about.

CHAPTER 32
PURPOSE

Although Maria started work at the cafe with the best intentions, it wasn't going very well. The manager and staff were kind to her, and Maria was very fond of them, but she was having trouble concentrating. She found it difficult to remember the relentless series of left-brained tasks.

One of the problems was Maria's ability to sense people's souls. She would become distracted by what she perceived around the customers and struggle to focus on the practical work. The customers seemed to sense her interest—perhaps because she couldn't help staring at some of them—and they often took the opportunity to tell her about their problems. But this was a cafe, not a healing room. The queue of tasks would grow longer. The manager was unusually patient with Maria, but the problem remained.

Back in Waldmeer Corner Store and Cafe, Maria's mother had provided a grounding influence that neither of them had fully appreciated. If Maria became too dreamy, her mother would quietly bring her back to the practical tasks, and Maria always obliged. Being mother and daughter, much was communicated without words. Lucy also knew when to leave her alone. If Maria was absorbed in conversation with a customer, Lucy assumed the person needed her daughter and would simply make things work around it. She gave Maria a great deal of leeway because she trusted her intentions. It was a good balance, and it worked.

The town of Waldmeer itself seemed to help. Its spiritual atmosphere protected Maria, whereas the city's energy appeared to do the opposite.

TWO LITTLE BLONDE SISTERS, four and five years old, often came into the city cafe with their parents. No one liked them, which is an unusual reaction to children. They were loud, obnoxious, and spoiled. They behaved somewhat better with their father, but when their mother was present, they were dreadful.

It wasn't that their mother didn't care about them. She talked to them constantly, read to them, played with them, and bought them treats and anything else they wanted. She was intelligent and polite, and she tried to correct their behaviour, but her pleas fell on deaf ears.

Maria felt sorry for them all.

When their mother wasn't looking, Maria would sometimes stare at the girls fiercely so they knew to behave better. They hated it, but because she also smiled at them whenever she had the chance, they did not avoid her.

"I don't know what to do," their mother said to Maria one afternoon as she brought her coffee. "The girls are not at school yet, and I have so much work to do. Every nanny leaves."

The mother was very good at her work and felt far more confident there than in her failing attempts at child-raising. The sisters, Marilyn and Bianca, were squabbling over their cakes, growing louder by the second. Suddenly the younger one stopped fighting, as if her mother's conversation had registered in her mind.

"I know, Mummy. Maria can look after us," said Bianca.

Everyone was surprised, but no one said no. They simply stared at Maria. Even the cafe manager, who had overheard the conversation, had stopped moving.

Maria turned to the manager. "Would it be all right?"

The manager tried not to look too pleased.

"We will miss you," she said, "but if they need you, we will manage."

She turned toward the kitchen and breathed out with a relieved smile.

Maria looked at the children, who were now strangely silent.

"Alright," she said firmly. "But we are all going to behave. Everyone is going to be good."

Maria needed a purpose for her work beyond simply making money. This family truly needed her, and that made all the difference. The mother could not have looked happier, and the family walked out of the cafe as if they were emerging from a fog.

TRUST

CHAPTER 33
NOTHING

Right from the start, Paul didn't like Maria. She had nothing against him, but we are careful with people who dislike us.

Gabriel had many gay friends in the city. It was a part of his life that Maria had not encountered before they became housemates. Now she occasionally met some of those friends when they visited the house. One of them was Paul.

Maria was sitting in the back courtyard, enjoying a patch of afternoon sun that had forced its way through the surrounding buildings. She heard Gabriel and Paul coming out of the house and was about to make her presence known when Paul suddenly stopped.

"Why is that girl from the country living here?" Paul asked.

"She's just a housemate," said Gabriel.

Something in Gabriel's voice surprised Maria.

Just a housemate, she repeated silently. *I thought we were friends.*

"She seems a bit strange to me," Paul continued. "And she has that room at the side of the house. What's that all about?"

"I don't know," said Gabriel, sounding uneasy. "It's nothing to do with me."

Nothing to do with me? thought Maria.

"You seem pretty buddy-buddy with her," Paul pressed.

"Nah, bro. I already told you," said Gabriel. "She just lives here. What she does or doesn't do is of no interest to me."

Paul took a few more steps, and Maria and Gabriel suddenly faced each other.

She made no attempt to hide the hurt on her face.

Gabriel looked mortified but quickly regained his composure. "Oh, hi Maria. We're just on our way out."

Paul showed neither surprise at seeing her nor any regret about what had been said.

THAT EVENING MARIA saw Gabriel in the hallway.

"Have you finished with the bathroom?" he asked.

"Yes, I have," said Maria.

She did not move from the doorway, and Gabriel eventually had to look at her.

"I'm not homophobic," she said, "but some of your friends are heterophobic."

"Don't worry about it, Maria. It's nothing," said Gabriel.

"You mean 'nothing' like I am to you?" she replied.

"I don't care how body appendages and holes relate to each other," she added with unusual bluntness.

"That's not very nice," said Gabriel.

It wasn't clear whether he meant it wasn't nice to talk about body appendages and holes, or that it wasn't nice to speak about his friends that way.

"You lot have made an invisible club," said Maria. "And if anyone questions its rules, the brotherhood turns on them. You keep token women as if to prove how well-adjusted you are. They might as well be trophy wives. You don't want equality. You want to be exclusive and special. But you are no more special than anyone else."

Gabriel turned and went downstairs.

A moment later Maria heard the front door slam.

CHAPTER 34

MAGIC MIST

Early the next morning, Maria was sitting on the bus to Waldmeer, staring out the window. The bus wove its way around the endless coastal curves. She opened the window slightly, even though the morning air was cold, and breathed in the fresh saltiness as if it were an all-purpose remedy.

Mist rose from the ocean in uneven clouds, drifted across the surrounding green hills, and settled again into a blanket of translucent magic hovering above the water.

None of the four of them had returned to Waldmeer since leaving six months earlier. Charlie—and therefore Gabriel—no longer had a house to return to. Maria and Mary, however, still had family there. Maria's parents belonged to a long line of Wald-meer dwellers, and Mary's parents owned the local dairy. Along with Mary's twin brother, Harry, the girls had been schoolmates since childhood.

They missed Waldmeer deeply, and for that very reason they had not returned. Waldmeer was in their blood. They had grown up nourished by its invisible energy, and life in the city was a sharp contrast. If they had gone back too soon, they might not have found the strength to return to the city again—although Charlie would certainly have come looking for Mary.

Maria had left a note on the kitchen table for Gabriel, Charlie, and Mary before she slipped out at five in the morning. She explained that the children she minded, Marilyn and Bianca, would be away with their parents for a few days, and that her mother could use some help at Waldmeer Corner Store and Cafe.

The rhythmic movement of the bus and the endless rolling of the sea had a calming effect on Maria, as it did on most people.

She did not exactly regret what she had said to Gabriel. There was truth in it, and some things need to be said. But she had been in the spiritual slipstream long enough to know that what she said was not the real issue.

It was not her calling to challenge the gay community. Their problems would not have upset her that much.

Gabriel's dismissal of her would have.

Anger is a cover for fear.

It was almost 8.00 a.m. when Maria saw her small hometown appear in the distance as the bus rounded the final coastal bend. She stepped off the bus as if re-entering a strange and irresistible world and walked toward the cafe to begin work for the day.

CHAPTER 35
SAFETY

Each day after work, Maria roamed the beach before trekking up the big hill to her parents' cottage. Wind, silence, waves, far sea—it was all beautiful. She wanted the conflict to bless her and not leave its mark without its benefit.

"Why are you being so dramatic?" asked Amira, whose voice had no static on the beach.

"I don't have many friends," said Maria. "The ones I do have are important to me."

Her few friends were carefully chosen, although not exactly chosen by her. She faltered as if searching for that point in the centre of a problem from which all the pain radiates. We must be brave enough to pull the simple, biting answer from the depths of our murky consciousness.

Maria saw a spurt of water in the ocean and knew a mother whale and her calf were out there. During winter and early spring, Waldmeer became a calving ground. Like other herd mammals, pregnant whales often isolate themselves and go to a safe place to give birth. The high swells, surrounding cliffs, and deep waters protected them from predators.

"If Gabriel feels pressured by other people," said Maria, "he will retreat into doing whatever seems least stressful and confrontational. He will not protect me."

She looked out to the mother whale, who was now playing with her calf, breaching and catching the sunlight on her massive, wet body.

"You are being too harsh," said Amira after a while. "You have been on the path a long time. You cannot expect Gabriel to know everything you know. It is only when we are far enough along to realise the sorry state most people are in that we lose our concern with what other people think of us."

The whales were quiet now. The sea was still as the gentle glow of dusk began pulling itself over the settling giant.

"It takes courage to tread one's course," said Amira, "but only at the beginning of each new stage. We hope that we are safe, but we are not yet sure. Go back to Eraldus. There is nothing to be angry about and nothing to fear."

Eraldus means *the dividing line.* Maria sometimes wondered what the dividing line was between. She would soon find out.

LANEWAYS

CHAPTER 36
BLOODLINES

Being an older inner-city suburb, Eraldus had many laneways crisscrossing behind the houses. Maria often walked them because they were much quieter than the streets. They were paved with uneven cobblestones and marked with weeds, puddles, graffiti, and solitude.

Eraldus had originally been a Greek area, and many olive trees and vegetable gardens still grew over and through the back fences.

In marked contrast to the stunning beauty of the Waldmeer beaches, the laneways were a kind of vacuum. There was little to look at, and so one began looking inward.

The energy in the laneways was different from that of the surrounding suburb. For one thing, Amira's voice was particularly clear there. However, other voices from lesser realms also seemed to make their presence known along the empty pathways.

It was a cloudy, cool afternoon with only occasional rays of sunlight. The laneways were quiet as usual, yet Maria kept feeling they were poised on the verge of action. Several times she turned a corner and thought she saw the fleeting movement of a group of dogs in the distance.

That was strange, because there were no stray dogs in Eraldus.

Maria stopped walking.

Something was there.

She could not see anything, but decided to head toward the nearest street and get out of the lanes. A woman stepped from the shadows and stood in the lane ahead of her.

Perhaps it is one of the elderly Greek women, thought Maria.

As she passed, the woman said quietly, "Why are you running away from me? I am your Great Aunt Evanora."

Evanora? thought Maria.

Yes, she did have a great-aunt called Evanora. She was one of the sisters of the great-aunt who died when Maria was sixteen. Maria had only occasionally seen the sisters and had always felt they were a strange mix, ranging from very good to very bad.

But which one was Evanora?

Evanora looked at Maria with eyes that were both vacant and full of vengeance. She pulled a gun from her coat.

A thunder of growls rose around them, and a great wind slammed Maria to the ground.

Galahad and part of his pack—about six male wolves from the North Country—were attacking Evanora.

Maria barely dared to look.

Although she was relieved to be rescued, the sight was deeply distressing. She sat motionless, unable to speak.

"Do not worry," said Galahad. "We have not killed Evanora. We have only destroyed her temporary form so she realises we are watching over you."

Sure enough, within moments the bloodied remains of Evanora began to dissolve and then disappeared completely.

"Would the gun have killed me?" asked Maria. "Was it real?"

"Your belief in its reality gave it some power," said Galahad. "We did not want to take that risk. One day you will realise that neither the gun nor Evanora has any power to harm you."

"Will she come back?" asked Maria.

"Not for now," said Galahad. "We are the guardians of your spiritual bloodline."

"Do you mean my family?" asked Maria.

"No," said Galahad. "Some members of your spiritual bloodline have appeared within your family line. At times there has been no one for generations. At other times, several have appeared at once. Whenever the light grows strong, darkness gathers around it."

"What about my great-aunts?" asked Maria.

"As you know, there were four sisters in that family," said Galahad. "One was the aunt who died. Another was the aunt who was upset with you for not visiting before her sister's passing. Then there was Evanora. She was placed within your bloodline to prevent the spiritual light of the youngest sister, Rose. Evanora watched her relentlessly, because she hated the light—and she hated Rose."

"What happened to the light sister?" asked Maria.

"She lived elsewhere," said Galahad. "She only recently returned to the Homeland."

Galahad then moved swiftly down the lane with his pack and disappeared.

CHAPTER 37
LETTER

A few weeks after the laneway experience, Maria sat at the table with Gabriel, Charlie, and Mary. Strangely, they were all there at the same time for dinner, which rarely happened. Maria was opening a letter she had received. It was the only letter she would ever receive in that house. She read it out loud.

> We want to advise you that your great aunt, Rose Este, has bequeathed her property to you at 6 Mir St, Eraldus. Once the legal documents have been signed, you will have sole ownership of the house.

Everyone was as shocked as Maria. They worked out that it was only a few streets away, so they walked there excitedly. The house was dark and covered with overgrown bushes. The vines had grown up the front of the house, made their home in the accumulated soil in the gutters, and were happily spreading out over the roof. No one could have lived there for some time.

The front gate had a tree trunk strewn across it, making it

impossible to open. They climbed over the gate, pushed through the bushes, and made their way to the front door. It was one of the original little council-owned houses in the area. Maria loved it instantly.

It was only a matter of a few months, and she had possession of the house, had done elementary repairs, and was moving in. Every day she worked there, Amira talked to her. Maria wondered whether this was Amira's house more than hers.

Amira told her that although she had two bedrooms, she shouldn't let anyone else live there. She was to use the spare bedroom as her healing room. Maria didn't know how to explain to her housemates that she couldn't share her house with any of them. She wasn't even sure why Amira wanted her to live there alone. In the end, she said little except that she was only a few streets away. Gabriel's friend, Paul, took Maria's room.

Maria was no longer a girl. She was a young woman with a house, a business, and a purpose. Yet, the child in us remains. It lives in our weaknesses. It lives in our trust. It lives in our desire to hold another's hand. It lives in our devotion to something bigger than ourselves.

CHAPTER 38
RETREAT

For the next few months, Maria went into an unintended but not unwelcome retreat. There was a lot of practical work to patiently attend to in the house. That kept her semi-focused on the material world. And she still had the children to mind. The care of two little girls also helped to keep her grounded. She saw her clients, but much of that time was spent in a healing consciousness. Apart from the children and her clients, she spoke to almost no one for the coming months. No one in this domain, anyway. She felt the house itself needed healing or enlivening. Her Great Aunt Rose would come and go, in spirit form, as if to check the progress of the house. Perhaps it was to check the progress of Maria.

Her healing room looked beautiful with little effort. It had a massage table where people could relax while Maria put her hands on them and prayed. They often fell asleep. The room had a soft light that seemed to say, *Relax, relax, everything is fine.* The scented candles flickered and filled the room with loveliness. Although Maria had not yet resurrected the garden, she found rose bushes under the rubbish. Most days, a little vase of roses sat on her table, reminding all that the world has such beauty. During this period, Maria became strangely unaware of her body. Yet, it functioned better than ever before. Usually, people have minor complaints about their bodies most of the time, if not major ones. Yet, her body seemed to have none. She often forgot about it entirely, and it seemed to forget about her.

The primary focus of her thought was forgiveness. It wasn't the forgiveness of trying to be nice to nasty people. That becomes passive-aggression or, at best, repression. It wasn't the forgiveness that says, *Even though you have done this, I will overlook it because I am better than you.* No, it was the forgiveness that alters our perception. It sees the spiritual truth and loses sight of the alternatives. Our ego refuses to do this because its main food is remembering the wrongdoings against us, even if they are entirely fabricated. To choose to see a different reality leaves the ego no room. It is the healing space. It is the beautiful space. It is the space of love and happiness.

Maria would not be left too long in her retreat, or it may become permanent. The hand of life would soon be knocking on her door, requiring her return.

MIR STREET

CHAPTER 39
BROKEN

Gavin was one of those good people who fixed up broken highchairs, broken families, and broken dogs. Semi-retired, all-round handyman, a little gruff as men that age often are, but sweet inside. He was one of Maria's Mir Street neighbours, along with his two dogs, whom he was tough on but adored—the perfect dog owner.

"Would you come with me to the pound?" asked Maria one morning as she walked past his house. "I have seen a dog there that interests me, but I need a second opinion. If you say no, then I won't get him."

~

WHEN THEY ENTERED THE POUND, Maria said, "By the way, he won't let anyone touch him."

Gavin frowned. He had a duty of care to give appropriate advice.

"What breed of dog?" he asked.

"German shepherd," said Maria, keeping up the casual style.

"An aggressive German shepherd?" said Gavin, as if he wasn't going to waste his time by going any further.

"Please, at least, look at him," said Maria. "They won't keep him any longer."

They both stood outside his cage. The dog certainly knew they were there, but he would not do them the honour of looking at either. He was matted and dirty because he wouldn't let the groomer touch him.

"He's way too big for you," said Gavin. "He will hurt you. Have a look at the other dogs. There are lots here that need a good home."

He would be a fine dog if he stopped fighting life, thought Gavin.

"His spirit isn't broken, but his trust is," said Gavin.

After Gavin left, Maria sat by the dog's door, waiting for him to show interest in her.

Gavin didn't exactly say no, thought Maria.

"Come on, boy," she said. "I'm your only chance. Take it. I'm on your side, but I won't force you. It is your choice for life or not. You will have to let me put the lead on if you are going to get out of this place alive."

The dog listened intently but suspiciously. Maria had been sitting on the floor waiting so long that she started daydreaming. She was surprised by a nose in her hand.

Thank God, she thought.

As she slowly clipped the lead to his collar, he suddenly bit her arm. A German shepherd bite is no little scratch. They can kill if they want to.

One of the pound keepers approached and asked, "Is everything alright?"

Maria quickly pulled her jumper over her arm and said, "All good, thanks."

This time, the dog let Maria attach his lead, and they walked to the office. She knew taking a dog that could attack was a great risk.

What if he attacked someone else? Yet, she also knew he wasn't bad, just broken.

Maria named him Gortaithe, which means injured in Irish. Sensing the risk she took to save him, he never again challenged her. He quickly gained a reason to live other than self-preservation. When we love someone, we make it our business to protect them.

CHAPTER 40

STEALING OR HEALING

"Hello, Verloren," said Maria, with surprise, as she opened her front door.

Maria was used to calling her Mrs Reisenden over the years of seeing her at Waldmeer Corner Store and Cafe, but she was too old to call her that now.

"I hope you don't mind me coming unannounced," said Verloren. "Your mother gave me your new address."

"It's fine. Come in," said Maria.

Verloren eyed the peeling paint on the walls and the bare, unpolished floorboards in Maria's lounge room. She turned her gaze to Maria and smiled.

"Your mother told me about your healing work," she said. "You probably don't know that I have a great interest in such things."

Maria was not so sure that the "such things" they were interested in were the same "such things", but she listened attentively.

"I would like to purchase a healing session," said Verloren.

"I see," said Maria. "What is it that you want healing for?"

"I didn't realise that one had to give a reason for wanting a healing," said Verloren, "but I am having a little issue with Farkas from Waldmeer. You remember him?"

"Yes, of course," said Maria.

"We had something of a falling out," said Verloren. "I am not one to hold a grudge, but I have recently seen him a few times in Waldmeer with a new female companion. It has come to my attention that he is moving forward, and as I have no other option, I need to set a few things right."

Maria knew Verloren was nowhere near ready to accept any true healing at this stage. Not only would it not work, but she would take whatever energy she could from Maria and use it against her at some future point. Further, Verloren's anger at seeing Farkas with a prospective partner would have ignited growing vindictiveness. *Hell hath no fury like a woman scorned.*

"I don't do healings on people unless I have worked with them for a while," said Maria.

Never one to accept *no* for an answer, Verloren said, "What is it that you would like to know?"

"Can you tell me why the falling out with Farkas is painful to you?" asked Maria.

For one brief moment, Verloren's face opened up like a window. There was no doubt her pain was substantial.

"I just wanted him to love me. Was that too much to ask?" she said.

Although she felt sorry for Verloren, Maria also knew she had much resilience in the face of pain and perseverance in trying to get what she wanted. Verloren needed a harsh awakening because nothing else would work.

"Yes, it was," said Maria. "It was way too much. Many women like Farkas. Why do you think he should love you over other women? Are you more beautiful, talented, accomplished, loving or wise? What were you going to give him that he actually wanted?"

Verloren was taken aback and scrambled for an answer, but

couldn't think quickly enough to find one. She was smart, but truth is smarter.

"You are being delusional," continued Maria. "I am not saying this to hurt you, but to help you. If you cannot face the obvious facts of the situation, you will never be able to move on to the deeper issues."

Verloren had already stopped listening. She was too angry. It is very confronting to be faced with our most treasured delusions.

She forced a smile and said as calmly as she could muster, "You are wrong, Maria. We were very close. He loved me. He just couldn't tell me, and now he has decided to look for someone else."

"You weren't close," said Maria. "He didn't love you. He used you for money."

Verloren was furious, but she pulled herself together, remembering the other issue she had come to see Maria about.

"You are entitled to your opinion," said Verloren, "but before I go, there is one other issue that I wanted to mention. I had a professional arrangement with Farkas about his garden, and he has not fulfilled his part properly. I was willing to let it slide in the hope that he would come good, but I believe there is little hope of that now. So I will be forced to use legal channels to right the wrong done to me."

She paused and added, "I don't normally repeat things, but I will tell you, in confidence, that he has said many bad things about you."

"Well, I'm sure he didn't mean them," said Maria.

Verloren stood up to leave and slid her expensive shoe along the rough floorboards.

"You look like you could use a little help restoring your house," she said.

"I like it like this," said Maria, walking Verloren to the door.

I can lie too, she thought.

CHAPTER 41

INEVITABLE BUT
NOT NECESSARY

That evening, Maria sat at the kitchen table with a cup of tea.

"I can't stand her," she said to Amira. "She's so damaging."

"Verloren is damaging because, like most people, she is damaged," said Amira.

Unlike Maria, Amira was never angry. She forgave everyone because she loved everyone equally. No matter what anyone did, she treated them like misguided children. Because of their problems, they were more to be loved and helped.

"The issue is not Verloren," said Amira. "It is your consciousness. Look at yourself. You are all worked up and keep rerunning the scenario in your mind, getting nowhere. Wouldn't you like to get your peace back? Wouldn't you like to feel happy again? Is the self-righteous anger worth it?"

IN TIME, Verloren would return. Time is not necessary for healing, but it is inevitable.

We find many friends when we are down and out. People swarm around with proclamations of, "Oh, how dreadful. How terrible."

They may as well say, "Thank you so much for making me feel better about myself and my life. You have more problems than I and are more pathetic."

Yet, when we enter the healing path, few will be standing there to wish us well, in case we find it.

MARIA OPENED the back door and looked into the clear, cold night. The moon was shining between the houses on its way into its rightful nightly place. She got ready for bed and listened as she lay her head on the pillow. The house was very still. The darkness was inviting and comforting, like a warm blanket.

She closed her eyes and said to the angels, "Take me somewhere beautiful tonight and teach me something wonderful. When I wake up, I will be happy and ready to share my happiness with anyone who would like it."

The darkness fell more deeply over her, and then the Light silently moved in.

CHAPTER 42
KISSING

*S*everal weeks later:
  The man bent over Maria and kissed her softly on the lips. He didn't wait long and kissed her again. It felt so nice. Warm and sharing. He wasn't taking anything, sucking the life out of her. He was joining with her, whole, unburdened. She slowly opened her eyes to look at his face. The early morning light was filtering under the curtain.

That's what kissing really is, thought Maria. *I don't care if it was a dream. It was a good one.*

"Do you remember the Jamiesons, the retired couple who came to live in Waldmeer a few years ago?" Maria's mother asked her on the phone that morning.

"Yes, why?" said Maria.

"I've sent a parcel of your things with their son, Richard," said Lucy. "He lives not far from you. He is an actor."

There were many actors in Maria's area, along with writers,

musicians, and artists. Gabriel and Charlie knew lots of them. There were healers, too, although Maria didn't seem to cross paths with them.

Richard knocked on the door a few days later. Maria couldn't remember him, but when she saw him, she wondered why—a good-looking man about ten years older than her, well dressed in an edgy actor sort of way, polite and quietly confident. He was slightly shy, making him all the more attractive.

"I don't think we have ever met," he said, holding out his hand. "Every time I visit your mother's cafe, she mentions you. I am on my way to get coffee now. Would you like to come?"

"Sure," said Maria. "I'll get my coat. I need a walk."

Maria didn't date. Men sometimes asked her, but she didn't take it up. Although she understood how the dating arrangement worked for other people, she found the idea illogical for her circumstances. Dates, as opposed to catching up with friends, assumed that one was available and interested in some sort of connection, ranging from casual sex to marriage and everything in between. Firstly, Maria didn't feel single. She didn't feel alone. The idea of searching for someone to fill a space didn't make sense to her. Secondly, she could read most people very quickly. The thought of dating a stranger in an awkward, draining, and undetermined situation to find out what sort of person they were (even though it was usually obvious) made her cringe.

Maria and Richard walked to the local cafe, which was buzzing with life. They immediately liked each other and found they had lots to talk about. After that day, they kept in regular contact. As much as Maria liked Richard and enjoyed his company, something about him made her hesitant to get too close. He was not pushing anything. He was too confident for that. He didn't need to ask women for anything. They usually made their intentions more than clear to him.

That's the problem right there, thought Maria. *I don't want someone to kiss me, like the man in my dream, and then think about kissing someone else in a year, six months, or six seconds.*

It was a compliment to have Richard's attention. However, a compliment is not enough. It has to feel right. It has to feel... necessary.

It wasn't long before Richard started talking about his new friend. Something in his voice told Maria that this relationship was important to him and was already beginning to change him, as genuine relationships do. Richard said that he would like Maria to meet his new girlfriend. He also said that Maria was the only person he had mentioned it to.

Why won't he discuss his new relationship with any of his friends and introduce her? thought Maria. *He is obviously falling in love with her.*

When they all met at the cafe, Maria understood why. She was expecting a woman like Richard, mid to late thirties, good-looking, vibrant, and confident. Richard walked in with his arm protectively around a woman probably fifteen years older than him. She looked good for her age, but Richard looked fantastic and was many years younger. This was not his usual style. Maria was intrigued. The woman was lovely but also strong and independent. No doubt she mothered him, but he didn't seem to mind. Then they would switch. Richard sat her on his lap and kissed her forehead. She laughed and didn't try to escape. He told her that she looked beautiful today. He was probably exaggerating, but no one cared. She did not need to be told she looked beautiful, but took it anyway.

The whole thing was delightful to watch. Maria felt happy for both of them.

She will give him all the love he needs, and her life experience will make her overlook many of his faults, thought Maria as she walked home. *But if he starts wandering or lying, she will be on it, sharp and*

short. She will remind him that he is free to walk out that door. It's
precisely the sort of approach Richard needs.

THAT EVENING, Maria asked Amira, "Am I on the right track to
think the way I do, or am I missing the boat?"

"Don't worry about that," said Amira. "It is not for you to
decide who you will love and trust. Love those who come into your
life. Love them for as long as they wish to be there. And then still
love them even if they are no longer there. You cannot run out of
love or give too much away. You don't have to decide or arrange
anything. Your happiness is already assured."

CHAPTER 43
GRACE

Maria had another Waldmeer visitor around the same time that Richard first visited. Mary's mother, Grace, had been ill and needed to see the city specialists. Gabriel was travelling and offered his room to Grace and her husband, Joe, for two weeks. Mary was worried about her mother, and Charlie was worried about Mary. It was a worried household.

Joe was a dairyman, through and through, and he had not been to the city for years. As much as he would do the right thing for his wife, he couldn't wait to get home. He was pacing the house so much that eventually, Mary told him to go back to the cows and that she and Charlie would look after her Mum. Joe was reluctant to agree, but he did. He couldn't help singing as soon as he hit the green pastures on the way home to his four-legged loves.

As Grace wasn't getting any better and the doctors didn't seem to make much difference, Charlie suggested that Grace visit Maria.

"What do you have to lose?" said Charlie.

Not only did Grace visit Maria, but she also told Maria that her house was the only place she felt less pain, so she came every day.

When Gabriel returned, it was arranged that Grace would stay in Maria's healing room for the rest of the month and that Maria would have a break from seeing other clients.

Maria asked Amira if she thought letting Grace stay was a good idea.

"Yes, it is," said Amira. "Grace wants to leave, so she has given herself a mysterious illness that will eventually get her that result."

"You mean leave life?" asked Maria.

"Yes," said Amira.

"Why does she want to go?"

"She has been unhappy in her marriage for a long time. She wants to leave her husband, but doesn't want to hurt anyone, and is afraid of the difficulties of such a big change. So instead of leaving Joe, she has decided to leave life, thinking that that will give her some peace."

"Is she conscious of any of this?" asked Maria.

"No," said Amira. "She has never been taught to understand her thinking and feeling processes and finds any self-analysis frightening and disturbing."

"Then we are starting at the beginning," said Maria.

While Grace was in Maria's house, she felt significantly better. However, Maria knew that without Grace's understanding of the underlying issues, her wellness would quickly deteriorate once she left. Each day, Maria suggested information to Grace about the possible thoughts underlying her illness. At first, she had to be very subtle because all Grace would say about Joe was that he was a wonderful man and that she was lucky to have such a great life. However, healing has its own power and once started, it moves ahead methodically, knowing exactly what track to take for the most efficient and effective results.

One evening, all of Grace's pain returned. Maria used the opening.

"You were just then on the phone with Joe, and he was talking about some of the things that you will need to attend to when you return to the farm," said Maria. "Do you think that your pain could, in any way, be related to your feeling about the farm, Joe, or your life in Waldmeer?"

Grace started crying hysterically.

Thank goodness, thought Maria. *She's getting somewhere.*

Maria calmly assured her there was nothing to fear and everything would be fine. Yet, at the same time, she could not miss this window of opportunity because they can be few and far between. Or perhaps it is our willingness to approach them that is few and far between.

"Imagine that your tears could talk," said Maria. "What would they say? Listen to them. They are trying to tell you something important."

Grace cried even more uncontrollably.

"I can't go back," she said. "I would rather die than go back. I feel trapped. I would so dearly love to live a little bit, live my own life, and learn about myself before I die."

"You can, Grace. And there is no need to die," said Maria. "Not for a long time, anyway."

Grace laughed out loud. It was a release. Maria laughed too. She had not seen Grace smile, let alone laugh.

"Perhaps, it would be possible to suggest a little break to Joe, and then you can see how things go," said Maria. "It doesn't have to be a big drama. There doesn't have to be any blame. Even if he gets upset and angry, keep loving him, and he will eventually see that you mean no harm to him, but you must also protect your life path. Your first responsibility is to your own worth. Everything comes from that."

～

GRACE RETURNED HOME TO JOE, but only briefly. A few weeks later, she rented a little flat on a pretty street near the river in the town closest to Waldmeer. It was a bigger town than Waldmeer, and Grace was delighted with all the opportunities it presented her. Joe was a complaining, bumbling mess when Grace left, but, to everyone's surprise, he pulled himself together after a few months and adjusted to life as a single man. He even asked a local widower out on a date. She was thrilled to have the company of an eligible man. She thought Joe was very handsome and manly. Joe was starting to enjoy life beyond his cows.

As for Grace, she was blessed beyond anything an onlooker could perceive. Even her daughter, Mary, did not really understand the change in her mother. Maria did. She heard it in her voice whenever Grace called. Maria knew the angels were blessing her, and she was becoming close to God. Her little bit of courage was greatly rewarded beyond anything Grace would have expected or even dreamed of. The return of her health was merely the first step.

After a while, Grace and Joe started to catch up for coffee in Grace's new town. Joe would dress up as if he were going on one of his, by now, many dates. They would sit in the cafe and talk about the family, the farm, and Waldmeer. This day, as they parted, Grace reached over and kissed Joe on the cheek. She had much love for him, yet she would never return. Something in the kiss shocked Joe.

"That is the first time you have voluntarily kissed me in ten years," he said quietly, wiping a tear from his eye.

He shuffled his feet and then walked off, saying he would pay the bill.

As they left, Grace turned to him and said, "Thank you for the coffee."

Joe stopped her. "No, Grace, it is I who must thank you."

He again started to cry and quickly turned for the car.

"I'll see you soon," he mumbled.

Straightening his suit jacket and tie, he waved as if he had many important things to attend to.

MEN

CHAPTER 44
HIERARCHY

Maria's dog, Gortaithe, was coming along well. He had relaxed into his inner-city household life, as relaxed as a German shepherd like him gets. He stopped looking aggressively at people and even let them pat him. He wasn't overly enthusiastic about human attention, other than his human, but he tolerated it with relatively good grace. Other dogs, however, were a different matter. Every dog was considered a possible life threat to Maria and treated accordingly. If Maria and Gortaithe walked the streets of Eraldus, he looked like a wild animal pacing the boundaries of his territory—head erect, ears up, leaning forward, eyes peeled. It was hardly pleasant to walk him and disconcerting to other dog owners. Walking the laneways, where dogs didn't tend to go, made life much easier.

It was a calm, bright autumn day with the type of mild, warming sun we crave after a bout of dreary, cold weather. Maria and Gortaithe approached the corner. A huge dog was off-lead and unattended. Maria panicked, expecting an all-out dogfight until she realised it was Galahad from the North Country. Instead of being his usual composed self, he seemed affronted.

"Who is this?" he said, looking at Gortaithe.

Gortaithe, for once, lowered his head, crouched, and backed away. Far from a wild beast, he seemed a boy in the presence of a man. Galahad was still not satisfied. He stared at Gortaithe, who knew to look away.

"Don't cross me," Galahad said to Gortaithe. "Ever."

Then he was gone as quickly as he appeared.

Well, I'll be, thought Maria. *Everyone meets their match or, in this case, superior.*

It only took a minute, and Gortaithe returned to his grandly dominant self, strutting the laneways as if he owned the world. Almost.

Ten minutes after returning home, Maria heard a knock at the door.

"Stay," she said to Gortaithe, who knew he had to sit at the far end of the hall although his spirit was bounding for the door.

It was Mr MacArthur. Maria hadn't seen him for years.

CHAPTER 45
TIME WARP

Mr MacArthur was the school principal of Waldmeer State Secondary School. Maria had known him throughout her entire schooling. When she was in primary school, he would visit assembly and give an inspirational talk which, for that age group, mainly consisted of reminding everyone to be kind.

He had been the secondary school principal for a hundred years—or so it seemed to the children. Even their parents could not remember a time when he had not held the position. As with many Waldmeer children, he had been one of the most important father figures in Maria's young life, second only to her own father.

"You have greatness inside you. I expect to see it," he would say at the secondary school assemblies.

Then he would add, with much gesticulation, "You are not just a small fish in a small pond. You can be a big fish in a big pond."

It was rather corny, and the students often rolled their eyes. But they heard it so many times that it became part of their consciousness during those formative years.

Having had no children of his own, Mr MacArthur considered

all his students to be his children. His wife had died about ten years earlier. He was highly community-minded and constantly winning awards for excellence. He was also forever trying to win awards for his students.

Somewhere along the way, however, he had forgotten that he had a life apart from school.

He seemed to have become stuck in a kind of time warp.

It wasn't the death of his wife that caused it. He just felt more comfortable in his work world, where he excelled. Outside that world, he did not feel the same sense of ease or purpose. Now, approaching sixty and facing retirement in a few years, he had no idea what would remain of him when work ended.

For this reason, he started doing a few things that he would never have considered before. They were small things, but they suggested that something long closed inside him had begun to open.

On such a whim, he decided to call at Maria's house the next time he visited the city. He did not bother ringing ahead. He intended only to stop briefly at the door to express his appreciation for Grace's recovery. Grace and Joe's twins, Mary and Harry, had also been under Mr MacArthur's care throughout their schooling, and he knew the family well.

"I bumped into Grace recently," said Mr MacArthur when Maria opened the door. "She credits her return to health to you. I simply wanted to say what a wonderful thing it is that she is well again—and that you must be an exceptional person if you can heal people."

Mr MacArthur was always the first to find reasons to congratulate others.

"Oh, how kind of you to call and say that, Mr MacArthur," said Maria.

"Please call me Thomas," said Mr MacArthur awkwardly.

"We are not at school anymore," he added, trying to sound funny.

It didn't come across as funny, but Maria laughed anyway.

"Okay, Thomas," she said with deliberate exaggeration.

They both laughed.

"Grace made herself well again," said Maria, "but thank you. I appreciate it."

"I won't keep you any longer," said Thomas. He paused. "I have decided I need a bit of a fashion overhaul, so I'm going to the shopping centre. I'm not very good at shopping, and I'll probably buy more of the same clothes I already have, but I'll try."

He said it without the enthusiasm he usually displayed in his assemblies about inspired living.

Maria glanced at his clothes. They certainly needed updating. They were ageing and dreary. She did not hold much hope for his shopping abilities.

At that moment Gabriel pulled up outside and jumped out of the car to drop something off for Maria from Charlie.

Maria introduced Gabriel and Thomas. Thomas would have been about the age of Gabriel's father, who had died when Gabriel was young. For some reason the two men looked at each other slightly longer than strangers normally would.

Maria explained Thomas's shopping venture.

Gabriel had a natural flair for clothes and enjoyed shopping. He looked at Thomas's outfit and almost screwed up his nose in disdain. Maria tried not to laugh.

"Tell you what," Gabriel said suddenly. "I'm going to the shopping centre myself. Why don't you follow me and I'll show you a few good shops?"

CHAPTER 46
UNLIKELY FRIENDS

When they got to the shopping centre, Gabriel pointed out a few suitable shops to Thomas and said goodbye. Thomas walked up to one of the chosen shops and looked like a fish out of water. Deciding that his old pond was the best option, he headed for the conservative old man's shop next door. He picked up one of the shirts on the rack. He couldn't remember if he had one like it or not. All his clothes looked the same, so it was hard to tell. Gabriel had been watching from a distance. Whether it was disgust or humanitarian aid, he walked over to Thomas and almost grabbed the shirt from his hand.

"It's horrible," he said.

Gabriel walked to the store he had originally suggested, expecting Thomas to follow. He had never been to Waldmeer Secondary School. Gabriel knew his new acquaintance only as Thomas, not Mr MacArthur, and treated him accordingly. Thomas stood blankly for a moment and then obediently followed. He was used to being obeyed, not obeying.

Walking around the shop with a bit of added drama for effect, Gabriel picked out all sorts of clothes for Thomas.

"Try these," said Gabriel, handing Thomas the clothes.

Thomas looked at them and hesitated.

"Look, I have other stuff to do," said Gabriel. "Do you want help or not?"

Then he added with a smile, "I think you need it."

Thomas bought it all, and they both walked out of the shop as if they had won a prize.

"How can I repay you for your help?" asked Thomas.

Feeling that the exchange was not quite finished, Gabriel said, "Buy me a coffee."

As if a barrier had already been broken, they started to talk about things that men don't easily talk about to each other. It was strange that they were so open, being virtual strangers, but many things in life are strange.

"I have decided it is time to get a new lease of life," said Thomas.

"I think I have had a bit too much of a lease of life," said Gabriel.

"What do you mean?" asked Thomas.

"I sometimes wonder if I am wasting my life," said Gabriel. "You have dedicated your life to people and your community. I wonder if I have spent too much of my life thinking about myself."

They seemed like opposites, but, on the other hand, they were alike—good men, well-adjusted, people-oriented, natural leaders, kind-hearted.

"I wish I had your sense of freedom and independence," said Thomas. "It would have saved me from many mistakes."

"What mistakes?" ventured Gabriel.

They had come this far, so Thomas decided to be honest.

"I have spent the last forty years of my life serving others. I do not regret caring about people and have gained many rewards along the way. However, I have also made many choices based on fear. I wish I would have had your courage."

"What sort of choices?" asked Gabriel.

"If I were braver, I would have left my marriage in the earlier years," said Thomas. "But I wasn't, and then the years go on, and it becomes too difficult to change anything. The trouble with staying too long with someone you don't want to be with is that you end up waiting for something to happen that will release you, even sickness or death. And then you feel bad that you could think like that, but what other choice is there when one is a prisoner? You would never let yourself get in that situation."

"No, I wouldn't," said Gabriel. "At least you weren't alone and lonely."

"It was intensely lonely," said Thomas.

"So is freedom," said Gabriel.

"But it's brave," said Thomas.

"Is it?" said Gabriel. "I don't know how brave it is. Maybe it's avoidance. That's not brave."

They both looked at each other, a little lost and forlorn. Being older, Thomas suddenly decided to change tracks.

"You know, Gabriel, I don't think either of us has been wrong," he said cheerfully. "In our ways, we have tried to find happiness. Yet, I don't think either of us is right either."

The waiter took their empty cups and asked if they wanted another coffee.

"No, I have to go," said Gabriel, still sitting there.

"I think there is a depth to life which only comes from our connection to other people," said Thomas. "However, we have to find it without becoming a prisoner. And we must believe that we will be okay no matter what. That gives us courage. I hope it will give me courage, anyway."

Gabriel got up, shook Thomas's hand, and said, "Enjoy your clothes and your journey."

He walked back into the busy shopping centre, but for some

reason, he couldn't remember what he had to buy, which was so important a few hours ago.

FROM THEN ON, Thomas didn't buy clothes without Gabriel. He would announce to his secretary that a particular day would be blocked out because he needed to see his stylist. He said the word *stylist* as if no one else would know what it was because he didn't previously know. Thomas and Gabriel became unlikely friends who would help to style each other's lives and thoughts.

BLISS

CHAPTER 47
BLESS

Maria threw her coat on the bed and turned the heater on. The house was cold on her return from the meeting.

"That was a disgrace," she fumed to Amira.

Gortaithe looked sympathetic. He would always be a one-eyed supporter. Amira, however, didn't say anything.

"Conceited, arrogant, egotistical, and delusional," said Maria.

She had been thrilled with the invitation left in her mailbox a week ago.

You are warmly invited to the first Co-operative Meeting of Eraldus Professional Healers, which the esteemed Bliss Kurt will chair.

Several semi-famous healers and self-help writers were living in Maria's area. Bliss Kurt was one of them. Tall with long, loose, blonde hair and excellent posture, she was an imposing figure. She had an equally good-looking partner, who Maria later discovered had only been around for the last six months. They looked like a cross between hipsters and movie stars.

Bliss was not precisely what Maria had hoped for, but she told herself that everyone is different. During a break in the meeting, she was in the bathroom when it was empty, except for, fortuitously, Bliss.

Great, thought Maria, *I will be able to connect with her when no one else is clamouring for her attention.*

However, Bliss took one look at Maria, acted like no one was there, and started preening in the mirror. After that, she seemed to have made a mental note not to look at Maria, let alone allow her to speak.

It wasn't exactly "a cooperative meeting of Eraldus healers". It was more of a presentation of Bliss's past achievements and future ambitions. Of course, such meetings are full of the words love, peace, and humility. There is an equal abundance of hugging, oming, and namaste-ing with hands prayerfully clasped together. Despite all the *love*, there seemed to be an uneasy feeling of spiritual one-upmanship. There was a lot of name-dropping.

One story that particularly annoyed Maria was Bliss's recollection of socialising with a world-renowned spiritual and self-help leader. "I'm not planning on coming back," he had apparently said to Bliss. He came from an Indian background, and the wheel of reincarnation was an inbuilt part of his view of evolution. "I want this life to be my last," he said. "I think I've done enough to warrant it."

Maria thought that anyone not coming back would not be talking about it. However, this man had done a lot to help humanity, so he was probably entitled to a bit of enlightenment self-promotion.

"I totally agree," Bliss had replied to him, all arms and drama. "I've done soo much to help the world that there is no way I am coming back."

You've done enough, thought Maria, *to promote your own pseudo-guruship to last several lifetimes. I am not sure how much you have actually done to help the world.*

The worst thing about the meeting was what Maria witnessed when she decided to quietly leave through the open kitchen door.

"Excuse me, Bliss," said a softly spoken woman in her fifties. "I was wondering if I could join the audience for some of the presentations."

She was wiping her hands on a tea towel after preparing food for the evening.

"Oh, sweetheart," said Bliss patronisingly. "You are coming along so well with your studies, but you are not quite ready to sit with the others. They are professionals, after all. I will let you know when it is time. Continue your service to the Divine, help me with the privileged work without complaint, and the Great One will bless you as it has blessed me."

Bliss then dismissed the woman with her hand as she was very busy. The woman didn't look in the slightest offended.

Maria continued walking through the kitchen. Just outside the door, a man was sitting holding his hand. He had burned himself on the stove. The woman came out to help him. She looked at him with as much love as if he were the world's most precious being.

She took his hand and said, "Edward, dear, don't be upset. There is nothing wrong with you."

The love and peace radiated from her, and Edward decided to jump up.

"You're quite right," he said as if he couldn't remember what the problem was. "I have things to do."

He happily returned to the kitchen, and the woman serenely followed.

Now, there's a real healer, thought Maria.

∾

"HEALING IS SIMPLE," said Amira that evening, as Maria complained to her, "if one is healed. The unhealed healer teaches what they live, which is the ego."

"It's my ego that is so annoyed with her, isn't it?" asked Maria. "Bliss is my peer, and instead of showing me respect, she acted like I didn't even exist."

"What else can get offended but the ego?" said Amira. "God is not a professional. Truth is not a profession. The spiritual path is more of an unlearning than a learning."

CHAPTER 48
LOVE FIRST, LOVE LAST

"It was a case of hot pants!" said John.

He was one of Maria's clients and didn't want healing. He just wanted to talk, so they decided to stay in the lounge room instead of the healing room. Before he started, he wanted assurance about confidentiality.

"It's a legal requirement," said Maria.

Satisfied, John explained that he was the CEO of a successful business and wanted his personal life to stay personal. He hadn't shared the issue with anyone, including his wife. Particularly his wife.

"As I said, my wife and I married young by today's standards," continued John. "We are only in our mid-forties but have been married for twenty-five years. Mostly, it was too much heat in the pants in our early twenties. Over the years, the passion turned into a respectful partnership, and we are still raising our children. I have been very busy with work and kids, and frankly, I never had much time for interpersonal mumbo-jumbo. I couldn't see the point until I met Sally two years ago. I don't know why, but I adore her. I think about her all the time. She has influenced my life in every possible way. Although I would not like to speak for her, I think she shares at least a little of that feeling for me."

John stared out the window. The climbing roses were creeping along the windowsill.

"I don't know what to do. I have a responsibility to my wife and children. And my marriage is...."

He searched for the word. What was it exactly? If he knew, he probably wouldn't be here.

"Serviceable," he said.

Maria laughed and said, "It serves a purpose."

"Yes, it does," said John, "and I don't want to hurt anyone, but I don't know that I will ever have an opportunity like Sally again. Not to be dramatic, but I feel I can't live without her. She has opened a door for me, and I cannot return to the blind way I seemed to stumble in the darkness before. It all seems somewhat meaningless now."

"Could you speak with your wife about it?" asked Maria. "Or begin the conversation, anyway."

"That might be the end of the marriage," said John.

"Maybe," said Maria. "Maybe not. Are you sleeping with Sally?"

"I know it seems strange," said John, "to love someone that much and not be intimate with them, but no, we are not. I am unwilling to take the risk that it would be the beginning of the end. The relationship is too important to me."

"It's not strange," said Maria, "and it means you haven't had to lie, which saves you a lot of guilt. Guilt is a slow killer. Better to learn how to be more open and let life take its course than live with lies. Lies rob us of our trust, and we project our untrustworthiness onto everyone around us. Have you ever noticed that the innocent are very trusting? They neither lie nor hold other people's lies against them. Liars, on the other hand, see sabotage everywhere." Maria paused. "Do you love your wife?"

"Yes, I do," John said without hesitation. "Not like I love Sally, but I do. My love for Sally is blissful." He smiled and added, "Maybe, blissfully crazy."

"Well, we do say we *fall* in love," replied Maria. "What can be reasonable or sensible about falling in love? It is crazy, high risk. It is also blissful because we see the divine in the other, and they give the same to us."

Maria stopped to let the divine presence settle into the room. She waited for John to feel the calm, reassuring energy.

"In love relationships," she said, "we become each other's teachers. Do not be afraid of love or the course it will take. There is no certainty in life. Choose love first and choose love last, and it will give you far more than you ever give it."

John stood at the front door and shook Maria's hand warmly.

"I was despairing," he said, "that there could be any right answer. I still don't have the answer, but I have a direction to go."

He looked at the wall hanging behind Maria. It read,

Except for love, nothing you see will remain.

CHANGE

CHAPTER 49
LOSS

For the past week, Gortaithe had not been himself. He was restless and jumpy. He kept barking into the empty night even though Maria assured him everything was fine and, when that didn't work, commanded him to be quiet. When they walked in the laneways, he wouldn't relax. He alternated between pulling on the lead and hiding behind Maria. Today was no different. A truck backfired, and he pulled so hard that Maria had to let go of the lead or fall over. Worse, he then ran off.

What on earth is he doing? thought Maria.

She ran after him and heard growling and snarling up ahead. The truck backfired again, and then all was quiet.

"Oh my God," she said. "No, no."

Gortaithe was lying in the laneway, soaked in blood, lifeless. Standing over him was Galahad, also streaked with blood. Maria couldn't understand what had happened, but right now, all that mattered was getting help for Gortaithe.

"It's too late," said Galahad. "He has gone."

"No," insisted Maria. "He can't go. It's a mistake. Bring him back. Bring him back."

Gortaithe and Galahad disappeared into thin air. All that remained was the warm blood spread over the cobblestones. Maria ran up and down the laneways calling Gortaithe. Perhaps, she had imagined the whole thing. The laneways were empty. When she got home, she rang the council and lost dog's home in case someone found him. She went into the laneways again. It was getting dark. She had to go home. After closing the curtains, she sat on the lounge and didn't move all night. Sudden loss has a way of immobilising us. Someone was at the door.

I must have fallen asleep, she thought with a start.

The doorbell rang again.

Perhaps, it's news of Gortaithe.

"Erdo!" said Maria, opening the door.

It was Erdo Kapus from the Leleks. Erdo reached out to Maria and hugged her.

She clung to him and cried, "It's my dog. I'm afraid he has been killed."

Maria first visited Erdo, her mystic teacher, when she was eighteen. She saw him a lot in those first few years, but less so once she moved to the back hills into Charlie's shed. She had not seen him at all in her two years in Eraldus.

"I know," said Erdo. "That is why I have come. Let me come in. I have brought you some food from my garden."

Erdo's food was not just nourishment for the body. It had healing properties. Nevertheless, Maria didn't want it.

"Oh, I can't eat," she said.

Erdo ignored her and walked to the kitchen as if he knew the house well.

"The dear old house hasn't changed much since your great aunt Rose lived here," said Erdo. "It got a little run down in her later years, but I see you are doing a fine job fixing it up again."

"You knew my great aunt?" Maria asked in surprise.

"Of course," said Erdo. "We all had a crush on her, but she

loved us all the same. Once, I almost convinced her to return with me to the Leleks, but in the end, she said it was unnecessary. I tried to tell her I thought it *was* necessary, but Rose was not the sort of woman one contradicts."

Erdo laughed affectionately. Many questions sprang into Maria's mind, but Erdo had busied himself putting the kettle on and placing a vegetable pie in the oven.

"Galahad did not kill Gortaithe," said Erdo. "I know you remember that Galahad warned Gortaithe not to cross him, but that was just a harmless warning."

He pulled out some homemade biscuits from his bag.

"We'll have these with our tea," he said. "It was Rose's sister, Evanora, who killed him. She has been walking up and down the laneways here in Eraldus lately. Gortaithe would have sensed her looming presence."

"Yes, he has been acting strangely for a week," said Maria.

"Gortaithe ran into Evanora in the laneway and lunged at her," said Erdo. "Evanora shot him. Galahad came as quickly as he could, but was not fast enough. Gortaithe died instantly, and Evanora disappeared back into the Shadowland. Because Gortaithe died protecting you, Galahad was allowed to take him back to the North Country."

"Is he in the North Country now," asked Maria excitedly, "with the wolf pack?"

"Yes, he is," said Erdo.

Maria was thrilled.

He will love it there, and he will be free, she thought. Another thought crossed her mind. *He can visit me in the laneways as Galahad does. Galahad often brings some of the male pack.*

"No, he cannot come," said Erdo, reading Maria's mind. "He has much training to do. He cannot move between dimensions. It is a learned skill. Also, Gortaithe's pull to this world will be strong for some time yet. If he returned, his attachment to you and his belief in this reality would make it difficult for him to leave this dimension. However, he would not be able to stay here for long. He would end up in the middle of the dimensions, stuck in the dividing line."

Erdo suddenly changed the topic and chatted about his recent forest visitors and students. He then got up and indicated it was time to leave.

Walking to the door, he said, "Gortaithe is not the only one whose path is changing."

CHAPTER 50
BIRTHDAY

"It's me, darling," said the early morning voice on the other end of the phone.

"Hi, Mum," said Maria.

"Happy twenty-sixth birthday," said Lucy. "I was going to post your present, but I also have preserves for you, which are too heavy to post. I made them from the last of our orchard's fruit. I saw Farkas the other day and asked him if he would drop them to you as he is travelling back and forth from Waldmeer, at the moment, for work."

"What sort of work?" asked Maria.

"Oh, who knows," laughed Lucy. "You know Farkas. He is so private. Dad says he could be a drug lord."

"I don't think he is rich enough to be running a drug ring," laughed Maria.

"Well, you never know," said Lucy. "Remember old Mr Perkins in the hills? We all thought he didn't have a cent to his name and often gave him things. Then, when he died, we found out he left a fortune to an estranged relative who also had no idea of his wealth." Lucy laughed at the memory. "Anyway, Farkas did reluctantly agree. Goodness only knows when he will turn up."

Lucy paused.

"We hope you know how much we love you."

"I do know," said Maria. "And I love you too. I could not have asked for better parents."

A FEW DAYS AGO, in Waldmeer:

"I remember when Maria turned eighteen and was working here in the cafe with you," Farkas told Lucy as she handed him the box of preserves and the present.

"Yes, that was eight years ago," said Lucy. "You had not long been in Waldmeer then."

"That long? It seems like yesterday," said Farkas, not wanting time to pass so quickly.

He was now in his late forties. A few more lines, but the same searching eyes. Since his winter in the North Country with the wolf pack a few years ago, he could see and remember more of the other dimensions. However, his recall was still very sporadic and unreliable. Sometimes, he thought he was drunk, and that's why he thought about such things.

CHAPTER 51
RELEASE

Maria sat in her lounge room looking into the green, still-overgrown garden. A candle was burning. She watched the flickering light as it unsystematically cast its mystery around the room.

I wonder how much of Amira is in me by now and how much of Maria remains, she thought.

One of the flame shadows subtly changed its shape, formed a face, and said, "It has been a long time since I spoke to you in the Homeland, asking if you would be willing to enter Maria's body as the Advisors had asked."

It was Milyaket, Keeper of the Vastandamine Forest.

"I told you that, at first, you would recall Maria's life, experiences, and preferences as if they were your own," she said. "Gradually, you started to hear Amira's voice. That began the transition from Maria to Amira. A slow transition was less stressful for you and your Earth parents. The transition has come to an end. Maria will no longer exist in this domain."

"What does that mean in practical terms?" asked Maria, for

once having a practical thought before any other, perhaps because it sounded like a life and death issue.

"Your questions will be answered more easily in the Homeland," said Milyaket. "We want you to lie your head on the lounge, breathe in slowly, and as you breathe out, we will gently take your soul with us."

THE FOLLOWING MORNING, Farkas pulled up at Maria's house on his way to work. He walked to her door with the box from her mother.

This box weighs a ton, he thought. *How many preserves does one woman need?*

Maria's front curtains were open, and he could see her resting. However, she did not stir even after he rang the doorbell numerous times. He put the box down and tentatively walked around the back. The door was not locked, so he walked in. Maria was unconscious but alive. He could not get her to wake up, but she didn't seem in pain or disturbed. She looked quite peaceful. He didn't have any idea what could be wrong and decided the quickest option was to take her to the hospital himself.

At the hospital, Maria was put on a drip and numerous monitors, and Farkas was told to ring her closest relatives. He rang the cafe because that was the only number he had. A stranger answered the phone. When Farkas asked to speak to Lucy, he was told that, sadly, Lucy had died peacefully in her sleep last night. He was also told that his wife's passing had given Lenny such a shock that his heart condition had flared up, and he was now in Waldmeer Intensive Care. The woman asked what Farkas wanted. He told her it was nothing, thanked her for the information, and hung up.

Farkas felt at a loss as to what to do. He left the hospital, telling the nurse he would return later. He put a message in Gabriel and Charlie's letterbox, knowing they would tell people about Maria.

Lenny never did find out about his daughter, not in this dimension anyway.

~

A FEW DAYS LATER, Farkas remembered leaving Lucy's box on Maria's front step. He drove there and took it inside. He opened the birthday present. It was a cushion that Lucy had embroidered. A note was pinned to it saying,

> *Maria, dear, I found this saying in one of your books that is still on the bookshelf. I'm not exactly sure what it means, but I kept thinking about it, and it almost embroidered itself on the cushion.*

Farkas held the cushion to the light. It read,

> *As you release, so shall you be released.*
> *Forget this not*
> *or Love will be unable to find you.*

He wasn't sure what it meant either, but Maria would know.

"Your mother made you this," he said to Maria when next he visited the hospital.

Maria was silent, of course.

"You will like it," he added.

He put it next to her head. He mostly visited the hospital late at night when no one was around. The night nurses at the desk tried to get him to fill out the visitor's forms, but he always made some joke and kept walking.

"You haven't filled out the visitor's form," a particularly officious, older nurse called to him. "Look here, young man, you must inform me about your relationship with the patient."

Farkas smiled at being called a young man. He continued walking and said over his shoulder, "Write that I am her brother."

CHAPTER 52
AMIRA OF ERALDUS

In the inter-dimensional Homeland:

Maria arrived in the Homeland bright and happy. That's the thing about the Homeland: once you are there, everywhere else seems miserable. Milyaket explained to Maria about her mother's passing and her father's imminent passing.

"Would you like to help them cross over?" asked Milyaket.

"Of course," said Maria.

"The Advisors have asked you not to speak to them," said Milyaket, "but to transfer your love and calm assurance that all is well. They are both confused by the transition and need time to adjust."

Maria was able to help her mother and, a few weeks later, her father over the bridge into their new state of mind. There was much for them to come to terms with. She silently walked with them, holding their hands—the hands they believed they still possessed—until they were more accustomed to life in the Homeland.

On Maria's last day, Milyaket told her that when she returned to Earth, she would have aged twelve years in terms of biology and demeanour.

"People who already know you will assume it is the result of the mysterious 'illness'," said Milyaket. "With time, they will forget what they thought you were and relate to what you are now."

That means I will be the same age as Gabriel and Charlie, thought Maria. *I wonder how they will react to that.*

"As you know, you will return as Amira, your natural self," said Milyaket. "However, like all souls that go to Earth, you will not be in your pure form. Your purity will be substantially dulled by entering Earth's lower base atmosphere. It will be a process of recall."

IN THE CITY:

Several weeks after being admitted to the hospital, Amira woke up. It was still dark, but the morning was not far off. There was enough light in the room to work out that she was in a hospital. She pulled out the drip and sat up. Once she adjusted to being vertical, she carefully put her feet on the ground and slowly walked over to the window. She recognised the city landscape below her. Home was not that far away. She left a note on the bed saying she would be back in the afternoon to check out of the hospital properly.

Some of her clothes were in the cupboard. She pulled them on unsteadily and walked hesitantly down the passage, past the desk, and out the glass sliding doors of the hospital. No one stopped her because no one was around. It was wonderful to be outside. Stretching her arms and back, she felt she was coming back to life.

I'm so hungry that I could eat a horse, she thought.

That was one of her father's favourite sayings when he returned from being on the fishing trawler.

I don't know about a horse, she thought. *Even non-vegetarians probably wouldn't want to eat a horse. This bakery has lights on.*

As she looked through the window, one of the bakers saw her and opened the door.

"Thank you so much," said Amira, taking away a bag of three croissants, a loaf of bread, and a bottle of milk.

She ate all the croissants and drank most of the milk. Now, she could think again. As she travelled on the bus to Eraldus, she tried to make sense of what had happened. How long had it even been? She did not know. She remembered sitting on the lounge in her home and Milyaket visiting. After that, she had no recollection of here on Earth. She did not know how she got to the hospital.

She could recall more of what happened in the Homeland. However, she felt that most of what had been conveyed to her would take a while to resurface in her mind. She did know, very clearly, that Maria was now gone. She knew her parents were safe in the Homeland. She felt no sadness at her recollections. She felt happy as she gazed out the bus window at the city houses with occasional early morning lights. Mothers of little children, shift workers, early risers, restless sleepers, and senior folk who don't need as much sleep anymore.

I am so blessed, she thought. *Everyone is so blessed.*

As she stepped off the bus, she realised that sunrise was close. The growing light made the footpaths clear.

"Hi, Maria," said Jack, the paperboy, delivering on his bike. "I haven't seen you for a while. Where have you been?"

He was a boy. No one would have troubled him with whatever had been happening.

"I was having a little holiday, but I'm back now," said Amira.

"Okay, great," said Jack, riding off as if it didn't matter one way or the other.

Fourteen-year-old boys have much more important stuff to think about.

Amira called after him, "By the way, my name is Amira now."

Jack momentarily stopped the bike and said, "My friend's Mum is called Amira. She says it means *one who speaks*. What are you going to say?"

He thought he had made the best joke in the world.

Amira laughed, "Whatever I am told."

HAPPY MOMENTS

CHAPTER 53
THE DANCE

"I'm not calling you 'Amira'," Gabriel said adamantly as they drove to their class. "You already have a perfectly good name."

"Okay," said Amira tolerantly. "It's up to you."

"And also, to be honest," said Gabriel, "I am not enjoying the person you have become in the months since your hospital stay. Frankly, you used to be much nicer."

Amira couldn't help smiling, but she covered it by turning to look out the window.

"I'm just getting older. We get more frank as we age," said Amira. "Perhaps, we are less tolerant of stupidity."

Gabriel didn't laugh at her joke. The only reason he stopped complaining was that they pulled up at the dance class. He was having trouble adjusting to Amira. It was a good sort of trouble. The kind of trouble that makes us grow. The trouble that brings the possibility of fertile, beautiful moments.

This was their fourth dance class. Gabriel had initially seen an advertisement for the class and asked Amira if she would like to go. Like most women, Amira jumped at the opportunity to partner dance. They were having mixed success. It wasn't the dancing—they could both dance—it was other issues.

"You are a *man*, and you can *dance*. That's double points," said Amira realistically. "You will be inundated with dance requests by all the women. You have a right to do whatever you want, but I don't want to dance with other people, and I don't want to sit here by myself. So, if you are not going to dance with me, I won't come."

Gabriel's response was a very reasonable affirmation of his intention to do as Amira asked. He was a reasonable man. However, the requests were mounting each week.

She would remind him, "I'm not coming if you leave me for ages."

"Okay," Gabriel would say, momentarily glancing at her. "I'll try."

Hmm, thought Amira. *"Try" is not what I'm looking for.*

However, the dancing would always save the situation. It wasn't all of the dancing. Much of it was spent with Gabriel telling Amira what she was doing wrong. It was the moments, the precious moments. The moments when no one was complaining, blaming, thinking about past hurts, or fearing future ones. It was those moments of simply being present to another person, moments of being grateful. Gratitude for another being, appreciation for life. Those moments made their relationship.

CHAPTER 54
HOME

Amira now had a car and could visit Waldmeer every weekend or so. She loved being home so regularly. Besides, there was much to do in caring for another house and garden. She put an ad in the local paper saying that a healer was available once a week in Waldmeer. She made the ad small, hoping conservative folk would not see it. Early on, she felt her parents in the house occasionally.

"Please don't feel you have to visit," she said to them, knowing that they would find a change of dimensions difficult and tiring. "As you can see, I am perfectly fine. I might not look after the house quite like you, Mum, but it's passable, don't you think? You both have other things to think about now. Don't look backwards. Look forwards. Besides, I will soon enough be with you."

Many of Lucy's friends no longer went into Waldmeer Corner Store and Cafe. Amira didn't go in either. One day, while in the other Waldmeer cafe, Amira saw Farkas sitting in the corner, reading the paper.

"Do you mind if I join you for a moment?" said Amira.

"Maria, hello," said Farkas. "How are you? Are you better now?"

"Yes, completely better," said Amira. "I haven't had an opportunity to thank you for taking me to the hospital. I eventually worked out who my 'brother' was."

"The nurse was insistent on knowing who I was," said Farkas, explaining nothing.

He didn't mention that he said he was her brother because Galahad had once told him that Maria was his sister under a different name. Everything about that was confusing, but Galahad was a male of fewer words than Farkas.

"I have a new name now," said Amira. "It's Amira. Do you like it?"

"Amira?" said Farkas. "Yes, yes, I like it. I like it very much. I used to have a friend called Amira."

He struggled to recall who that friend was. It was not only Farkas who couldn't remember his long-ago association with Amira; it was Amira, too. As a human, many things disintegrate when one enters the Earth's atmosphere. Memory is one of them.

"We are closing now," said the waitress.

They walked out of the cafe into the late afternoon. It was the end of winter. They could hear the ocean rolling in, unrelenting and unconcerned with the fast-fading light.

A seriousness grew over Farkas's face.

"I hate winter," he said. "Sometimes, I hate Waldmeer."

He might as well have said, *I hate myself,* but he stopped before those words had a chance to come out. Amira touched his hand.

"Please stop hurting yourself," she said. "That voice you listen to is no friend. It promises so much, but when has it ever given you what it promised? When has it ever given you any happiness longer than a fleeting moment? It has your destruction as its goal, not your happiness."

Farkas put his hands in his jacket. He didn't want to hear such words, but the trouble with words like that is that once heard, they become implanted in our minds. There they grow, whether we like it or not. The road is inevitable for anyone who ventures near it.

"It's not as dark as last week when I was here," said Amira. "The days are getting longer. The cold will be gone soon."

"I'm glad you are better," said Farkas. "I'll go home now."

"Yes," said Amira. "So will I."

TOGETHER (BOOK 2)

PART I
TOGETHER IN WALDMEER

ALAMGIR

CHAPTER 1
CONQUEROR OF THE WORLD

Amira hadn't had the nightmare since she was twenty. Back then, she was known as Maria. The nightmare hadn't crossed her mind during the two years she had been living in Eraldus. Now that she was travelling back to Waldmeer each weekend, it was occasionally returning.

That was strange because nothing could be more charming than Waldmeer—going to sleep to the distant sea, waking to forest birds, walking to the rhythm of the breaking waves.

Some years ago, Maria came face to face with the malevolent nightmare when she went to see her teacher, Erdo, in the forest. That was the first time Amira spoke to her, and the beginning of many years of instruction.

Now, Maria was back in the Homeland, and Amira had sole charge of the body they had shared. Some years had been lost in the transition, and Amira was in her late thirties, though she seemed somewhat ageless.

~

"ERDO, is that you? What are you doing here?" said Amira when coming out of the Waldmeer Post Office.

There before her was a smiling Erdo. He was dressed like one of the local dairy farmers, complete with muddy boots and felt hat. She had not seen him since her weekly return to Waldmeer, although she thought she saw someone who looked like him a few times. It dawned on her that it must have been Erdo all along.

She recalled that he looked like a forty-year-old businessman with an Armani suit and slicked-back hair last week. Another time, he looked like a retired city dweller visiting his holiday house, with less hair and plumper than the previous sleek version. Yet, it was the same unmistakable Erdo expression—a cross between amusement, exasperation, and compassion.

"I have come to see you," said Erdo.

That's a privilege, thought Amira. *Erdo rarely leaves the forest. His students go to him.*

"Let's walk," said Erdo. "Do you remember before your twenty-first birthday, you met Alamgir?"

"Alamgir?" asked Amira, recalling no one of that name.

"Yes, Alamgir," said Erdo, "the darkness from your nightmare that day in the Leleks."

"Oh, is that its name," said Amira.

"Yes, it means *conqueror of the world,*" said Erdo.

"I hope it isn't," said Amira, pulling a face.

"No, but it tries," said Erdo. "It takes every opportunity it can. The few years you have been away from Waldmeer in Eraldus, it has been winning quite a bit."

"Can't you stop it?" said Amira.

"I am not allowed," said Erdo. "The Advisors of the Homeland forbid interference with human choices. It is how humans learn. They must sleep in the bed they make until they make a different one."

"I see," said Amira.

"One day, everyone will realise that they don't even need a bed," laughed Erdo, "because sleep is a respite from a tiresome world made up of the problems created in the day."

Come to think of it, Amira had never seen Erdo's bed and, for that matter, never seen his house. He had always just appeared in the forest after she crossed the old walking bridge next to the peaceful pond with the black swans. She looked up at him to ask about his house, but he was gone.

CHAPTER 2

DEMOLITION

T homas was tearing out pages from the local Waldmeer paper to use as kindling for his fireplace. He glanced at one of the pages and saw a small advertisement.

Healer available in Waldmeer on weekends. Call Amira.

The address given was Lucy and Lenny's old house.

Maria must have changed her name to Amira after her parents died, thought Thomas. *I guess Amira is a more exotic name than Maria for a healer.*

He imagined a crystal ball and heavy, closed curtains. Healers were not exactly his style, but for some reason, he stuck the ad on his fridge. That morning, Thomas had stopped his car at the end of his street outside Kathleen's house. The bulldozers were there. The house was already half demolished. He sat transfixed as if the machine was methodically ripping out pieces of him with each assault on the house. He couldn't bear to watch it, nor could he drive away.

"You better hurry up, Mr MacArthur, or you'll be late for your own staff meeting," yelled one of his young teachers as he drove past on the way to Waldmeer State Secondary School. "I can run it if you like."

Thomas waved him on with a forced laugh and started his engine again. He knew by the time he drove home, the last trace of Kathleen would have vanished. It was painful. He didn't want to go to school. He didn't want to go home. He just wanted to crawl up in a little ball and die. How could he have let this happen? He didn't even know how it happened.

CHAPTER 3
KATHLEEN

Tall and slim, with shoulder-length, slightly curly hair, Kathleen was always beautifully groomed, although she never looked *groomed*. She just looked beautiful, as if she had woken up like that. Possibly, she did because she rarely wore makeup. She had more than a touch of the wild woman in her. She was never happier than on the beach with the wind wreaking havoc with her curly locks. She didn't hide from the sun, so her face had a healthy glow. She was willing to accommodate the lines in return for the benefits of being outside. Anyway, she owned her lines. They added to her appeal as if to say, *Don't mess with me. I'm no insecure young kitten.*

Kathleen's husband was a prominent doctor in the city. He had an extensive career, and part of his work was with the underprivileged. Although Kathleen had spent most of her time raising children, running a busy home, and supporting her husband, she was no second fiddle. Accomplished in her own career before children, she was a constant source of wise advice to her husband and contributed greatly to his professional success. They had more than enough money for their needs, but refused to live in one of the city's wealthy suburbs. They did, however, allow themselves the luxury of a holiday house in Waldmeer. They bought it more than twenty years ago. It was a few houses away from Thomas and his wife.

Kathleen and her husband did not enjoy the company of Thomas's wife. She was the opposite of Kathleen. Short, fine-boned, and fragile. She complained about the sun and equally complained about the cold. She always seemed ill in some way, if not physically, then emotionally. Whereas Kathleen's attractiveness seemed to grow with age, the years were not kind to Thomas's wife. Perhaps she was not kind to the years. In retrospect, she even seemed old when they all first met and were less than forty.

Thomas's wife often remarked, "Marriage is for life. These days, people seem to have no loyalty or perseverance."

Kathleen thought, *People who have the most to gain out of a relationship are the ones who say, "Marriage is for life, no matter what." They say it as if they are so virtuous when, really, they are warning their partner that if they leave, they will be held accountable.*

It was enough to keep a man like Thomas in check. Thomas worried about what many people thought, not just his wife. There was no question of leaving.

As tedious as it was to tolerate Thomas's wife, it was easy to love Thomas. He was their first friend in Waldmeer, ensuring all the other locals accepted and welcomed them. He kept an eye on their house when they were in the city. He was a genuine and good person devoted to his school and community. Thomas couldn't help but secretly fall in love with Kathleen. He probably fell for her the first time they met, but he wouldn't allow himself such thoughts. Besides, he was as much in awe of her marriage as he was of her. It was so honest and productive. Kathleen and her husband were true friends and survived the ups and downs of life and marriage with the grace of two well-balanced, focused, and altogether lovely people.

Thomas's wife often seemed on the verge of a life-and-death sickness. Eventually, she got one that killed her. Several years later, Kathleen's husband, who had rarely been ill, died from an unforeseen medical issue. It was only natural for Thomas and Kathleen to continue their friendship.

CHAPTER 4
SHORT SKIRTS

"You are punching above your weight," joked a friend to Thomas as he and Kathleen walked into the restaurant for dinner.

Thomas knew he was. He was so thrilled to be in a relationship with Kathleen. When Thomas first asked Kathleen, she was hesitant, but seeing his need, she accepted.

Although Thomas was thrilled about the relationship, almost no one else in Waldmeer was. They were used to him being with an ineffectual person, not someone with Kathleen's dignity and intelligence. It seemed to them they had much to lose and little to gain.

Alamgir whispered into their ears, and they heeded him. They could not hear the other voice—that Kathleen had their best interest at heart.

The first outright enemy was a young teacher at school with short skirts but big ambitions. She was an attractive woman in her early thirties—highly manipulative, with Thomas easily wrapped around her finger.

Over a few years, she had wooed, flirted, and seduced her way into the top spot of his favourites. Although Thomas told himself she was a great asset to the school, everyone could see he had been hoodwinked.

Of course, Kathleen realised this instantly and tried to help Thomas rectify the situation by putting the girl back in her rightful place. The girl's eyes were glued on the prize of easy power, and she would have none of it. Thomas, she could handle. Kathleen, she could not. Kathleen had to go. It was a matter of survival.

The young teacher lied her way through the teachers, school administrators, and townsfolk. Her malice matched her ambition. People knew she was a liar, but they were intimidated by Kathleen and preferred the girl's seductive foolishness to Kathleen's self-assurance and courage.

Alamgir was delighted with the choice.

The school and townsfolk refused to invite Kathleen to events as Thomas's partner, even though everyone else was invited. Thomas said nothing. They would walk past, paying their respects to him and giving Kathleen a sour smile, if anything at all. Thomas said nothing. He should have fired the girl, but he wouldn't. He did nothing.

In the end, it was the girl who held all the firepower.

CHAPTER 5
FIRE

One evening, Thomas couldn't sleep. He was sitting on his balcony listening to the night sounds, wondering what to do about the situation with Kathleen, which had been escalating. Just as he got up to go back to bed and wrestle with sleep, he looked over to her house. He could see the furthest point of her back garden from his balcony. He was startled to see a flame.

Maybe it's a light flickering, he thought.

It wasn't. It was a fire, and it was rapidly gaining momentum.

Oh no, Kathleen's back shed is on fire, he thought.

He ran barefoot up the street to her house while dialling the fire brigade.

"Kathleen, wake up. There's a fire in your backyard," yelled Thomas as he banged on her front door.

The Waldmeer Fire Department didn't often have emergencies. In a relatively short time (for a department unused to emergencies), they were there with hoses and extinguished the fire.

"I'm sorry, Kathleen," said the head of the department, "but this was no accident. Someone poured petrol on your shed and lit it deliberately."

Kathleen and Thomas knew who it was. The girl had many young male fans in Waldmeer, any number of whom could have carried out a favour in the hope of a return one.

That was the end for Kathleen. She knew that to continue would end in her own destruction. Thomas either couldn't or wouldn't stop it. She told herself that he couldn't, but somewhere in her heart, she wondered if it was that he wouldn't. The next morning, she went to the real estate agent and asked him to put her treasured holiday home up for sale.

"I think it's for the best," said the real estate agent in a kind, resigned manner. "You have a wonderful life in the city. You don't need us. It is we who could have benefited from you."

In the end, few were Kathleen's friends—few, indeed.

The young teacher remained at Waldmeer Secondary School. Thomas told himself that it was best to keep the peace and not cause any more trouble.

Alamgir laughed.

CHAPTER 6
CONQUEROR OF NOTHING

Kathleen's brother was a Zen Buddhist monk. He lived in the hills, outside the city, and helped run a retreat centre. Now that Kathleen no longer had a house in Waldmeer, she visited him weekly to have contact with nature and solitude. His monk name was Aishi, meaning *compassionate service*. He was true to his name.

"They were so damn mean," said Kathleen to her brother as they walked along the winding path of the hermitage.

After listening for some time, Aishi asked, "What is it that you want? An apology?"

"Apologies are cheap,' said Kathleen.

"What is it then?" asked Aishi.

Kathleen stopped walking and looked at her brother. "It's Thomas," she said. "I want to know I didn't waste the last few years of my life."

Aishi smiled. He had the serenity of one who lives as part of nature's ongoing, never-failing transformations.

THAT EVENING, in Waldmeer, Thomas stared at the ad on his fridge.

Healer available in Waldmeer on weekends. Call Amira.

It had been a gruelling day after watching the demolition of Kathleen's house.

It's worth a try, he thought, not knowing what else to do.

A few days later, in Amira's lounge room, Thomas said rather awkwardly, "I suppose you have heard about Kathleen and me."

"We are a small town," said Amira.

"Don't believe everything you hear," said Thomas.

His words rang hollow.

"I don't believe everything I hear," said Amira in a tone that surprised Thomas. "She was a gift to you. I hope you looked after her."

"Of course I did," said Thomas, unsure of the direction this was going.

He attempted to tell the story in more detail. Amira was silent.

Eventually, he blurted out, "I just want her back."

"Kathleen is not coming back," said Amira. "Why would she? You were willing to take everything she had, which was a lot, and then let the wolves eat her so long as they didn't eat you."

Thomas was shocked by Amira's bluntness and what she was implying.

"Are you suggesting I wanted to hurt her?" he said.

"I am saying that you wanted to use her for your advantage without paying the price," said Amira.

"What sort of person would do that?" said Thomas, not waiting for the answer.

He stood up to leave.

"Thank you for your assistance, but I won't be requiring your services anymore," he said as if firing an out-of-line employee.

Amira knew she was being tough on him, but she had to be. This was his chance. Otherwise, he would slip into the next few decades with decline and loneliness as his companions.

Thomas gave Amira her money and abruptly left.

~

TWO WEEKS LATER, he was back.

"I have been through every emotion," he said wearily. "Mostly anger. I was angry that you implied I could be so selfish and gutless."

Amira remained quiet as she was not sure where he was up to in his healing.

"It took me a week to stop being furious with you," said Thomas. "Then I started to feel terribly sad and, worse than that, guilty. I still feel overwhelmed with guilt, and I will probably never be able to get rid of it."

"Don't get bogged down in the guilt," said Amira. "It is as egotistical as the anger. The ego is fragile and brutal, and no one is safe from its betrayals. It will always choose what it thinks is in its best interest, for the cheapest price. It may be as blatant as short skirts and lies, or hidden behind kind words—but it comes from the same place: using people to get what we want, or trying to remove those who stand in our way."

"I don't have anything else but school and Waldmeer," said Thomas by way of explanation. "The last thing I wanted to do was hurt Kathleen, but I can't afford to lose the only thing I have."

"If that were true, then your choice would be understandable," said Amira. "However, what you are holding onto is quite worthless. You must already suspect this, or you would not have come to me and certainly would not have returned after the first bruising visit."

They both laughed.

"Although Kathleen was a gift to you," said Amira, "learning this is a greater gift."

As Amira waved to Thomas from the front gate, she looked down to the beach at the bottom of the street. The sunlight was playing on the water.

"You are not conqueror of the world, Alamgir," said Amira. "You are conqueror of nothing."

BUNGALOW BUDDIES

CHAPTER 7
TRANSLUCENT MAN

The past few weekends in Waldmeer, Amira had been seeing a man out of the corner of her eye. She could tell the man was no longer an Earth resident because he was translucent. That made it easy!

He was about her age. Tall, blonde, broad shoulders like a footballer. Amira felt that it was not her that he wanted to speak to. She guessed he wanted to communicate with someone in Waldmeer who couldn't see him. She had no idea who, but life always has a way of telling us what we need to know.

IDE LOOKED at his sleeping body. She loved those strong, broad shoulders. It was not only a beautiful body, but so far, it had proved itself to be a resilient one after all that he had put it through. Fabian's body was not yet showing the ravages of recurring addiction.

He was probably more at home in his body than anywhere else in this world. His mind was fractured. His spirit fragile. Yet, his body had always served him well. In sports, in love, he radiated physical health and competence.

She wished he would not destroy his beautiful body with a sick mind, but knew it was only a matter of time. After waking up, Ide realised she had been dreaming again. Fabian died eight months ago.

Not long after their baby was born, Fabian went to jail for a drug-related offence from his younger years. Ide lost him to prison for three years. When he returned, he was good for some years, but the addiction kicked in again. He was in and out of rehab.

He was killed in a car accident earlier this year. He was drunk. This time, she and her boy lost him permanently. No one said it, but many felt his death had freed Ide and her by now twelve-year-old boy to have a normal life.

Ide appreciated their concern, but they did not realise, and perhaps could not, that Fabian paid for Ide's love with his own. As broken as he was, he loved her.

Ide looked at the other Waldmeer women and rarely saw in their husbands' eyes the devotion she saw in Fabian's. That was worth a lot. There was no need for pity because Ide knew she had been loved.

CHAPTER 8
ENERGY FIELD

One Saturday afternoon, Ide made her way to the meeting she had been invited to. She didn't want to go. She was still grieving and didn't want to do anything, but she was told that the meeting organiser had a bright money-making proposal. Ide needed the money. Amira had also been invited. There were fifteen other people present.

When Amira walked into the room, she noticed a woman about her age with fair skin, calm blue eyes, delicate features, and a gentle energy field. She had occasionally seen the woman around Waldmeer but knew nothing about her.

"Hello, I'm Amira," she said, sitting beside the woman.

"I'm Ide," said the woman. "Nice to meet you."

"Ide? That's an Irish name. That explains your looks," said Amira, smiling.

"Welcome to the first meeting of the Bungalow Buddies," said a friendly, round woman in her early sixties. "As you are probably aware, seventeen of the houses in Waldmeer have an identical bungalow on their property. They originally came from the old hotel near the pier, where seasonal workers once stayed. When the hotel no longer needed them, the bungalows were offered to locals—provided they moved them themselves."

Amira remembered how her (Maria's) father had jumped at the opportunity and enlisted his fishing mates to haul the bungalow up the hill into their back garden. It still sat there twenty years later on rough blocks of tree trunks, the floor slightly uneven but workable.

"A few bungalows have gone to rack and ruin," the meeting convenor continued. "One or two have been updated and are now quite fancy. However, I understand that most of them are substantially unchanged and empty. I'm sure that together we can do something lovely and constructive with our bungalows."

The woman's inclusive, good-willed nature quickly won everyone over.

After a pleasant meeting, the convenor said, "We will meet again in a month. Good luck with fixing up your bungalows and finding tenants."

CHAPTER 9
BE THERE

Charlie and her partner, Mary, had been living in the share house in Eraldus for more than two years. Charlie had decided it was time to sell her property in the back hills of Waldmeer and buy a house in the city with Mary.

It was only a few years, but it felt like a lifetime (perhaps a different lifetime) since Amira had driven up the long, dirt driveway of Charlie's property in the back hills. She parked outside her old shed, which Charlie had affectionately named *Maria's Shrine*. She peeked in as she walked past. There was nothing in it except a few items on the windowsill. Farkas had been renting Charlie's property since his return from the North Country. Amira hadn't let Farkas know she was coming. She didn't have his number. Anyway, she felt it was best to catch him off guard. She took a deep breath and knocked on the door. Nothing. She was fairly sure that he already knew she was there. He had eyes like an eagle and a sixth sense to match. She decided that the best option was to wait patiently. That way, he would know that she was not kidding about wanting to talk to him. Somewhat resigned, he came to the door.

"Hello, Amira," said Farkas. "It's been a while since you have been in these parts."

"Yes, it has," said Amira.

Farkas didn't invite her in.

"I know it's none of my business...' said Amira.

That was a mistake. She immediately felt Farkas prickle.

"Charlie told me she is selling her property and already has a buyer who wants to live in it," said Amira. "Obviously, you will have to move soon."

"And?" said Farkas. "Your point?"

"I have a friend who lives a few streets from me," said Amira. "She is at the bottom of your old street."

"Go on," said Farkas.

He must need somewhere to move, or he wouldn't let me continue, thought Amira.

"I know it's not much," said Amira, "but she has a bungalow and needs someone to rent it. It's cheap."

"Why are you interested in me living there?" said Farkas, not one to beat around the bush. "I'm sure you are aware that I am quite capable of finding my own accommodation."

"Of course you are," said Amira, trying to soften him.

Farkas was unimpressed.

"Why?" he repeated.

Amira said honestly, "My friend is a lovely woman. She has a son who is twelve now. They have been through a lot. The husband had a problem with addiction. Not long after their boy was born, he went to jail. Later, he was in and out of rehab. Eight months ago, he was killed in a car accident. I know he brought it on himself, but he loved his wife and boy, and they loved him."

"Well, I'm sorry for them," said Farkas, "but I don't see what it has to do with me."

"I thought that if you lived there for a while," said Amira, "it might help them by having a man around the place. You wouldn't have to do anything. Just be there."

Amira paused and then said more bluntly, "Maybe care. That would help."

"Thanks for the suggestion," said Farkas, "but no thanks. I have enough of my own problems."

He put his hand on the doorknob to indicate it was time to go.

Amira didn't budge.

"Look, Farkas, it's not just them. It's you. Do you intend to be a hermit for the rest of your life? It's not good for you."

Farkas stared at Amira and spoke down to her, "I have told you before that my life is none of your business. What I do or don't do has nothing to do with you. I can't make this any clearer than I already have."

Not quite ready to concede defeat, Amira said with quiet determination, "You are not the only one suffering. Don't you think you could reach out to someone else and help a bit? You might even find it gives your life some meaning."

Time to go, thought Amira.

She didn't bother saying goodbye. The time for niceties seemed to have been over a few moments ago, probably after the first sentence.

CHAPTER 10
DONE DEAL

"Hi, Gabriel," said Amira, answering her phone. "How are you?"

"Hi Maria," said Gabriel.

He still wouldn't call her by her not-so-new name of Amira.

"I haven't seen you much lately," said Gabriel. "You have been in Waldmeer a lot."

"Do you miss me?" said Amira.

"No, no, it's not that," said Gabriel.

Amira smiled.

"Now that Charlie has sold her property, I have been thinking how much I miss my trips to the back hills of Waldmeer," said Gabriel. "It was so good for me as an artist. The peace and quiet inspired me in a different way from what I get in the city. It was special."

"Yes, it was a special time," said Amira, thinking of it fondly.

Both were silent for a moment, and then Amira suddenly said, "I have an idea. Why don't you rent my bungalow? You can set it up as a studio. You can have cheap rent because when I moved to the share house in Eraldus, you helped me for a whole year."

"Done deal," said Gabriel without hesitation.

In the space of a few moments, a new happy plan was set in place.

AT THE NEXT Bungalow Buddies meeting, the convenor asked each resident how they got on with finding a tenant.

Ide spoke when it was her turn, "I have someone, thank you."

That was all she said. She wasn't a big talker. Amira briefly saw the translucent man standing behind Ide with his hand on her shoulder. As Amira had by now suspected, it was Fabian. She could not tell Ide that he had been around lately, but one day, she would. That was the last time Amira saw Fabian.

"That's wonderful news," said the convenor. "Everyone in the Bungalow Buddies has managed to find a renter."

A sense of accomplishment fell over the group. By working together with a gracious spirit, they had quite easily created something that would benefit everyone.

"Until next time, my friends," said the convenor.

A ray of goodness spread out from the little group into the town. Amira walked up to Ide and put her arm through hers on the way out of the meeting.

"Buddy," said Amira, smiling.

"We *are* buddies," said Ide, "bungalows or not."

She held onto Amira's arm more tightly than she needed to.

"So, who is your tenant?" said Amira.

"The guy from Charlie's property," said Ide.

"Really?" said Amira.

"Yes, I was a bit surprised," said Ide. "He called at my house and said he had heard I had available accommodation. I showed it to him and told him the price. He said it was too much for an old bungalow. When I replied that he could have it for half price if he fixed it up a bit, he said he would take it."

"That's great," said Amira.

"He did add that he wouldn't be there for long," said Ide.

"It doesn't matter. It's all good," said Amira. "Anyway, time will tell."

"I hope we don't bother him," said Ide, a little worried. "He said that he is used to keeping to himself. I don't want my son to start annoying him."

"Oh, don't worry about that," said Amira. "I'm sure you will both do him a world of good."

Ide is more polite than I, thought Amira. *Farkas will find it easier to cope with her.*

There was something else Amira wanted to find out.

"Do you feel okay about him being there?" said Amira. "I mean, not everyone in the town likes him. Do you?"

Amira looked directly at Ide and waited for the answer. She knew that instinct was the great director in the formation of all relationships.

"For some reason," said Ide, "I do. I don't know why. I just do."

"Then," said Amira, "it's a done deal."

REACH FOR IT

CHAPTER 11
DONE OR DIFFERENT

Amira carried the last art supplies from Gabriel's car down the winding track to the bungalow. He had been driving to Waldmeer the previous few weekends as he was keen to fix up the bungalow as a country studio.

"Thanks a lot, Maria," said Gabriel. "Anywhere on the floor is fine."

"Okay," said Amira. "I'll leave you to it. I'm sure you have lots to do."

She turned for the door, which was only two steps away. The entire length of the bungalow was no more than ten steps, probably eight of Gabriel's. It was just enough room for a bed and a small kitchen table. One single cupboard and sink made up the kitchen. Next door was a tiny room with an old but adequate bathroom. Running along one entire wall was Gabriel's art and sculpting equipment.

As the floor was uneven, he had bits of wood underneath everything. The wood was constantly reshuffled to stabilise the structures.

Amira looked back as she closed the bungalow door, expecting

Gabriel to be staring at his works of art, all at various stages of completion. She was surprised to see that he was, instead, staring at her.

She stopped walking and asked, "How's it all going? Are you happy with what you are making?"

"Truth be told, I'm not. I don't know what's wrong exactly, but I'm not happy with any of it," said Gabriel.

Amira stepped back into the room and touched some of the clay. It was harder than she expected. He must not have been working with it for some time.

"I feel that most of my best work was done a few years ago at Charlie's property," continued Gabriel. "Maybe, I'm done."

He sat on the bed in exasperation, throwing his arms in the air and falling back.

"Maybe all the art in me is used up. I'd better think of another job fairly soon, or I might have to live in this little bungalow permanently."

Amira laughed and said, "Don't worry. I'm sure you won't have to live here like the local fringe dweller."

She walked over to the window. The wood around the frame was worn and rough, but serviceable. In the distance, she could see the ocean between the trees. It looked still and calm from up here.

"Perhaps, you are not 'done' but different," she said. "You are not the same man you were a few years ago. Maybe you need to find out who you are now."

"That could take a long time," said Gabriel.

"What is the problem, exactly?" asked Amira. "Is it that you can't think of what you want to create, or don't like anything you make?"

Gabriel pulled himself up off the bed.

"If I start working on a piece the way I used to, before long, I feel as if it's..." he paused as he searched for the right word. "You know I'm not good with words."

He slumped back on the bed.

"Your words are fine. Reach for what it is you want to say," said Amira.

After a moment, Gabriel said, "Empty," with the irritation of someone who had discovered an unwelcome visitor living in his house.

"Empty?" said Amira.

"Not enough," said Gabriel, still annoyed at his discovery. "What once seemed enough doesn't seem enough anymore."

"That's because you've changed," said Amira. "What satisfied you before doesn't satisfy you now. You have more in you, and you won't feel right unless you find it—and express it."

"How do I do that?" asked Gabriel. "I've tried, but I seem to get nowhere."

"Be braver. Be more honest," said Amira. "Don't hold onto what you used to know. You're an artist—you're meant to express what other people can't. What's true for you now will take more courage."

CHAPTER 12
WHO ARE YOU?

The next day, Amira was packing to return to Eraldus. Gabriel walked up the hill from the shops and sat on the grass beside her car.

"Are you also leaving this afternoon?' asked Amira.

"No, I'm going to stay a few more days. I need some more time alone."

"I wish I could stay here in Waldmeer, too," said Amira. "These days, I feel so at peace here that I have to make a big effort to go back to the city."

"You are peaceful whether you are here or in Eraldus," said Gabriel, not entirely pleased with this observation. "Do you even need anyone else in your life?"

"Is that why you won't call me Amira? Because you think Amira doesn't need anyone and Maria does?"

"Sometimes, Maria was strange," said Gabriel unapologetically, "but I felt that she was, sort of, manageable. Now, I'm not sure I even know who you are."

He looked down at the grass and wondered if he would regret those words.

Amira did not want to dismiss his words lightly. They had a lot of truth in them. She was very different from the girl he first met years ago, and even very different from the prehospital-Homeland transition eight months ago. She wondered what she could say to acknowledge his feelings, but let him know it was nothing to be concerned about. There was much she would love to tell him, but she could not. He would not understand it. And far from reassuring him, it would scare him. Suddenly, the seriousness left her. She smiled, walked over to Gabriel, and took his hand.

"We are both here, aren't we?" said Amira.

Gabriel didn't know what she meant or how that was supposed to make him feel better. Amira hugged him and got in the car. He didn't hug her back because he already felt too vulnerable.

CHAPTER 13
IT'S GOOD

I t was Wednesday night.

Three days on, thought Gabriel, *and I haven't thought of a single creative idea.*

He turned the light off and lay in bed. He didn't bother closing the curtain as no one could see in. However, he could see out.

His eyes accustomed themselves to the dark. The mass of luminous stars started to make their presence known. The longer he looked, the more radiant they became.

Before closing his eyes, he sent a request to those majestic stars: *You light-bringers that give so much, why don't you tell me what I should bring?*

~

In another dimension:

What is this place? Gabriel wondered as he found himself amongst grand trees, luscious grass, dazzling water, and sublime colours.

There was an overriding feeling of beauty, synchronicity, and happiness everywhere around him.

He was vaguely aware that it was a dream, but it was so vivid and meaningful that he didn't care what it was.

For several hours, he was completely immersed in a sense of wonder and deep satisfaction.

THE LAST STAR bid its farewell as Gabriel looked through the bungalow window. It was morning, and he was awake.

Wow, that was astonishing, he thought. *I hope I don't lose the memory of it.*

Instinct told him to stay close to nature to hold onto it for longer. He walked down to the town, and everything looked brighter. He passed several young boys, laughing and chasing each other with their skateboards. They seemed so full of joy. The shopkeepers and customers all seemed happier than ever he had seen them. The morning could not have been more perfect.

Turning his mind to work, he noticed that the effects of the previous night were already starting to fade. He knew it was a temporary offering from the stars, yet the dream still had such a palpable residue in him that he wondered if he had somehow misunderstood life in all his previous years.

Perhaps we are mistaken, he thought, *to think our life is so concrete and material. I have never felt anything to have more reality, vibrancy, and importance than I did last night.*

Instead of turning to his sculptures, Gabriel went to the cupboard and pulled out a canvas and oils. He had not painted for many years. The painting seemed to paint itself. In one day, he had substantially completed the most impressive artwork he had ever done.

Even if no one else likes it, I know it's good, he thought.

By Friday morning, Gabriel's normal consciousness had, for the most part, returned. It was inevitable, and he didn't begrudge it. As he was packing up to leave in the afternoon, a neighbour walked to the front gate.

"You must be Gabriel," said the woman. "Amira told me that you are in the bungalow. Is she back from the city yet? I want to let her know about the upcoming church fete."

"Not yet," said Gabriel. "She will probably be a few more hours. I will let her know that you called."

Gabriel folded the note letting Amira know about the neighbour and started to write *Maria* on the outside. He remembered the dream, crossed out *Maria*, wrote *Amira* instead, slid it under her door, and headed back to the city.

THE CONVENT AND
THE CLINKERS

CHAPTER 14
THE CONVENT

Amira's neighbour had recently let her know about the forthcoming church fete and festivities to commemorate the one-hundredth anniversary of the Convent. It was a place Amira loved. Inscribed on the heavy wooden door of the Convent were the words:

Built on the hill to be close to God.

It wasn't difficult to find a hill in Waldmeer.

Originally, the order was enclosed. They did not interact with the outside world. Their life was prayer. Amira felt the very air inside still carried the sacred energy of their prayers. She didn't go there too often. She had to remain in the world.

In the early days, the nuns grew much of their own food in a large garden. The priest would take the excess each Friday and sell it at the weekend market, along with the sisters' candles.

Whenever Amira visited the Convent, she passed a row of paintings of the founding sisters. The one in the middle was Sister Geraldine. Something about the pictures fascinated Amira. She often said hello to them by name as she passed. Even she didn't expect them to answer. But one day, Sister Geraldine did.

She told Amira that she had come from Ireland.

"I told God that if I could be of service to anyone in the world, my soul would be happy," said Sister Geraldine. "He brought me here to Waldmeer."

Although the order was enclosed, Sister Geraldine said that, eventually, it was time to educate the children of the logging families.

The day came when the sisters would step out into public life.

The nuns always sat behind a curtain in the church, unseen by the congregation. One Sunday morning, the sisters walked into the curtained area and sat down as usual. Then Sister Geraldine stood up and, with a touch of drama, opened the curtains. She had a sense of humour.

The congregation collectively gasped as they witnessed the unveiling of the holy sisters.

The sisters got the giggles.

And so began their public life of service.

And serve, they certainly did.

CHAPTER 15
THE CLINKERS

Although the sisters were now educating the children of Waldmeer and the surrounding areas, they were forbidden to teach the Clinker children who lived in the back hills. Their camps shifted with their parents' movements. The instruction came from the Bishop, and the sisters were bound to obey.

The Clinkers had appeared in Waldmeer around the time of the forest loggers. They were a cross between gypsies and monks. Although they were a deeply spiritual people, it manifested in ways foreign to Waldmeerians—dancing, chanting, magic, healing, living in nature, and free-spiritedness.

The women usually wore red veils in town, with lots of jewellery and small, clinking bells. That was how they came to be called the Clinkers. No one thought to ask their real name. The townsfolk preferred the nickname. It carried the suggestion of belonging in jail.

Many were suspicious of their magic and healing, and some of the Clinker boys would steal from the townsfolk. The boys were quick and stealthy—no match for townspeople. The elders tried to keep them in line, but every group has its trouble spots.

Sister Geraldine was fond of the Clinkers and possibly a little envious of their freedom. She would have loved to run barefoot through the forest, sing with the trees, and befriend the creatures.

At one point, six Clinker children were brought to the Convent by their mother. She refused to speak to anyone except Sister Geraldine. The children were fatherless, and the mother was ill. She said she was going to the city for treatment. She did not want the children to be raised by the other Clinkers. She wanted them educated, not raised only in the ways of the forest.

Sister Geraldine explained that she was not allowed to take the children.

The woman, who read minds more than she minded words, looked at Geraldine with the determined eyes of a forest creature protecting her young and said, "You are their mother now."

She then left.

Sister Geraldine told the other sisters that the children were orphaned from a Waldmeer farming family. Everyone knew it wasn't true, but Geraldine wanted to spare the sisters from breaking their vow to the Bishop. She felt bound to a higher order.

The other sisters were thrilled to have children living with them. After all, they would have been mothers if not for their religious decision. They immediately got to work and enclosed the long verandah, scraping together six makeshift beds.

The children slept in those beds for three years.

Then, their mother returned, and the children needed to go back to their family. The youngest child was only a toddler when she first came to the Convent. She did not recognise her Clinker mother and refused to leave Sister Geraldine, whom she considered her rightful mother.

Sister Geraldine kept taking the child to her mother in the back hills, gradually getting her used to her biological family.

Each time she returned alone, the other sisters knew not to ask. They all missed the baby.

The little girl spent much of her childhood returning to the Convent. As an adult, she emigrated to Ireland, Sister Geraldine's homeland. There, she married and had children of her own. Eventually, she had ten grandchildren.

The youngest of them was Ide!

Ide had no idea of her connection to the Convent or Sister Geraldine as her adoptive great-grandmother. Certainly, she never dreamed she had Clinker blood in her.

All of this was told to Amira, piece by piece, whenever she passed Sister Geraldine's painting in the Convent hallway.

Amira had to think of a way of telling Ide without saying, *Oh, by the way, I've been talking to your dead, adoptive great-grandmother, and she wants you to know who you are.*

Like Sister Geraldine, Amira decided that a white lie was preferable to a fatal truth, so she told Ide she had found the Convent records and read about Ide's ancestry there.

Thus began Amira and Ide's frequent visits to the Clinkers. They usually visited on ceremony nights and couldn't have had more fun with all the dancing, singing, laughing, magic, and healing. It was very theatrical, but most religions carry a good deal of drama.

The Clinker blood in Ide was thickening with remarkable speed.

CHAPTER 16
LITTLE LIGHT

I de mentioned the Clinkers to Farkas, expecting him to have no interest. To her surprise, Farkas told her he had also been spending time with some of the Clinkers. She had never seen him there and didn't understand why he would be. He was not religious or spiritually minded, nor one to go looking for friends, and the Clinkers were not an obvious choice.

Ide never questioned Farkas. Whatever he chose to tell her was enough. Having Farkas in the bungalow was working well, and Ide did not want to sabotage it. Not least because her son, Christopher, was becoming attached to him.

Christopher would stride down the driveway to the bungalow with legs that seemed to grow an inch every week. Ide sometimes worried that he would be broken-hearted when Farkas decided it was time to go, but she had known enough loss to understand that holding back from life's joys for fear of their ending only means missing them.

Although Ide never questioned Farkas about his association with the Clinkers, she did ask one of her Clinker girlfriends.

"Oh, yeah," said the friend, "he's been hangin' out with *the lost ones.*"

"The lost ones?" queried Ide.

"Himach and that lot," said the friend, "those weed guys. The elders call them *the lost ones* because they say that they have taken the freedom of the Clinkers and turned it into trouble with their drug-taking and irresponsible ways. They are the ones giving the Clinkers a bad name. Farkas is an adult. He is free to make his own choices, but if I were you, I'd make sure they don't get their hands on Christopher. Some of our teenage boys have lost their way through them. They waste years of their lives telling themselves the drugs do not affect them, while all along, they are sedating themselves for much of their waking lives. The elders say they are wasting the gift of life and that it is an insult to the Great Life Energy."

Remembering the Clinker code of love, she said, with sadness in her eyes, "I get angry with them, but it is because they are my brothers. I've seen too many of them destroy themselves."

That evening, Ide saw Farkas in the back garden and said quietly, "I don't want Christopher near any of those Clinker weed-boys."

There was a determination in her voice that surprised Farkas. It was the same determined voice of the mother who had once left her children with Sister Geraldine (Ide's biological great-grandmother).

"Relax, it's only marijuana," said Farkas. "It's not like a real drug."

Ide cut him off. "I don't want Christopher in the bungalow when it's there."

Farkas shrugged and walked off as if it was a fuss about nothing, but he knew she was right. At that moment, a little light of love for Ide grew in his heart.

CHAPTER 17
SECONDER

"I'm sorry, Amira, but unless you have a seconder, the matter cannot be put before the assembly," said the Convenor, knowing full well that no one would second it.

Amira was at the meeting for the upcoming one-hundredth anniversary of the Convent. This would be the year's social highlight for Waldmeer, so it was not just church people who were present. Business owners, council members, townsfolk, and those associated with the Convent were all there. Everyone was represented except the Clinkers. One had to have an invitation to attend, and they were not invited.

Amira knew they wanted to be involved and decided it was time to press the town on this divisive issue. However, she couldn't find a suitable seconder for the motion, which meant it could not even be tabled for voting.

"I will second it," said a strong female voice up the back.

Amira couldn't see who it was, but the voice sounded familiar.

The Convenor looked stunned but composed himself and said, "Alright, your name, please?"

"Verloren Reisenden," said the woman. "My husband and I

have a holiday house here in Waldmeer. I will second Amira's motion."

No one was more shocked than Amira. As it unfolded, it was due to Verloren that there was a positive outcome for the Clinkers. It was not just that she had made it possible for the motion to be put before the assembly. That was the first step, but it was still unlikely to pass. Verloren was no fool when it came to people politics.

"You may be aware of the successful business my husband and I run in the city," said Verloren. "As is appropriate these days, we always have a policy of inclusion regarding such matters."

Whether the townsfolk knew of her business or not, they could tell that Verloren was a woman of means and business standing. Whatever she said, they were willing to accept in acknowledgement of her superior judgment in the situation.

If Amira alone supported the Clinkers, the people would have dismissed it as the peculiarities of a well-meaning but incomprehensible person with a questionable profession. If she weren't a local, born and bred from good ol' Lenny the fisherman, she would have probably been lumped in with the strange Clinkers.

"Thank you, Verloren," said Amira after the meeting.

Amira knew it was a fragile situation and that Verloren could easily return to her previous hostile position, so it seemed best to say little.

Verloren dismissed Amira, saying, "I don't like nastiness. Besides, the Clinkers are known to me personally."

None of that had much truth in it. Verloren didn't like nastiness towards herself, but she could be as nasty as the best of them. Nor did she know the Clinkers personally. She may have had a vague knowledge that the Clinkers were somewhere in the hills, but she would neither have understood nor had any alignment with their type of spirituality. However, it didn't matter.

What did matter was that Verloren had decided to use her

considerable personal magnetism and force-to-be-reckoned-with nature for a good cause. It was, indeed, a surprise that the good cause was Amira.

"I heard Farkas is living at the bottom of my street," said Verloren tentatively.

"Yes, he is," said Amira. "Close to his old house, where you are now. He's at Ide's."

She wanted to add, *But don't go there. It can only lead nowhere good.*

Instead, she touched Verloren's arm lightly and said, "You look like you are doing really well. So, whatever you are doing, keep doing it."

UNFORESEEN
CIRCUMSTANCES

CHAPTER 18

LAUGHING AT A FUNERAL

"Guess what, Amira," said Gabriel excitedly on the phone.

"I don't know. It sounds good," said Amira, enjoying Gabriel's happiness.

"Come on," urged Gabriel. "You're a healer. You're supposed to be psychic."

"Only sometimes," smiled Amira.

She had no idea what his good news was, but not wanting to spoil his fun, she ventured, "Hmm, my powers are telling me that..."

She paused, waiting for a suitable idea to pop into her mind.

"You sold your painting for a large fortune."

"Nope. Guess again," said Gabriel.

"For a small fortune?"

"No, not even close," said Gabriel, getting annoyed that she wasn't on the same thought track as him.

"What is it then? You will have to resort to telling me," said Amira.

"I got married!" beamed Gabriel.

Amira almost dropped the phone.

Married? she thought incredulously.

"Isn't it wonderful?" purred Gabriel.

"Yes," said Amira weakly. "But to who?"

"What are you talking about? To Paul, of course," said Gabriel.

When Maria/Amira moved to Eraldus a few years ago, she shared a large inner-city house with Gabriel, Charlie, and Mary. When Amira inherited a rundown house from her deceased great-aunt Rose, she moved into it, and Paul took her room in the share house. Paul was one of Gabriel's gay friends. Amira recollected that Gabriel and her worst argument happened when Paul had manipulated Gabriel into saying that Amira meant nothing to him other than as a casual housemate. The memory of it still had some sting.

"I see," said Amira, searching to make sense of what Gabriel was telling her.

How could I have missed this? she thought. *What else have I missed?*

"You sound surprised," said Gabriel.

"I knew you were dating him," said Amira, "but I didn't realise it was so serious."

"Why wouldn't you realise?" said Gabriel. "We have been together since you moved out of the house."

"You rarely talk about him," said Amira. "So, I thought he wasn't that important to you."

"Well, he is. He is my husband," said Gabriel. "You are not being homophobic, are you?"

"That's silly," said Amira. "You know that I don't see people as bodies. You are entitled to everything that everyone else is."

You are entitled, she thought, *to all the same stupid mistakes as everyone else.*

In another world where communication is transparent and honest, Amira would have been able to say, *My concern has nothing to do with sexual orientation. My concern is that I don't think you love him. Not enough, anyway.*

Unable to say that, Amira could think of nothing else to say.

Breaking the uncomfortable silence, Gabriel said, "We love each other, have great fun together, our interests are the same, and seldom fight. We aren't that young anymore. After speaking about it, we agreed that there is no one else for either of us and that we should take the plunge and start making memories together as a team."

"That's great," said Amira, not accustomed to outright lying.

"Don't worry, we'll still have lots of time together," said Gabriel. "Paul wants to come with me whenever I travel to Waldmeer so the three of us can spend time together when we are there. It'll be a bit squishy for two people in that little bungalow. But, hey, we are newlyweds. It'll be cosy."

Amira laughed. It felt like laughing at a funeral.

"I look forward to it," she said.

The last thing she wanted to do was spend time with Gabriel and Paul together. She had to search for qualities in Paul that she liked, and did not like the person Gabriel became around him. She pulled herself together, feeling that any moments spent with Gabriel were precious and fast declining.

"Thank you for telling me," said Amira. "I appreciate it. I'll let you go now. I'm sure you have lots to do."

It was a defining moment for Amira, one of those surprises life can throw our way that leave us searching for meaning. She got off the phone and walked to her favourite chair. It was the one where she read and prayed, where the angels gathered. She sat down and cried.

CHAPTER 19
TURNAROUND

Although with Verloren's unexpected intervention, Amira had a victory with the church council about the Clinkers, it was short-lived. Less than two weeks later, she received a letter from the town council telling her she could no longer practice as a healer in Waldmeer.

The town protocol clearly states that no one is to conduct a business that is seen to undermine the reputation of Waldmeer as a leading tourist destination. As numerous residents have complained about the appearance of an unprofessional business of dubious nature, we regret to inform you that you cannot conduct your business as a healer in the vicinity of Waldmeer. We trust that you will cooperate with our instructions immediately. As our decision is final, we will not enter into any further correspondence.

Cowards, thought Amira. *Do I not have the right of reply? And what complaints? From whom? Is the council calling me a charlatan?*

She knew that they were repaying her for helping the Clinkers. Courage always has a price. It doesn't come for free. It was a large price, but Amira felt it was not for her to say what it would be. With a heavy heart, she took down her sign from the front gate and told herself that she would have to be satisfied with her practice in Eraldus.

Amira told Ide about the letter from the Council. Ide, in turn, told Farkas. Farkas, in turn, told the Clinker guys he had been seeing lately. For all their faults, *the lost ones* were not lost in every way. They were men with the fire of *this will not do* inside them. Generally, however, it tended to get focused in the wrong direction. Not this time. The Clinker guys decided, with Farkas, to approach the Chairman of the Council. They knew where he lived. It was dark and quiet as they stood at his door one evening. The Chairman was far from at ease when he opened the door to the wild-looking Clinker men. He went to shut the door, but Farkas came from the back of the group and put his foot in the doorway.

"They have something to tell you," said Farkas.

The Chairman recognised Farkas from town and visibly relaxed.

He looked at Himach, the Clinker spokesman, and said, "What is it then? What do you want from me?"

"We know the trouble with Amira is not about her," said Himach, "but us. If you let her have her practice and don't stop our mothers and sisters from being involved with what they want in the town, then we will move on."

"Will you?" said the Chairman, thinking this would make many townsfolk happy.

"Not all of us," said Himach. "Just us young guys. We are the ones you don't like. Leave our families to live in peace, and we will go to the Flatlanders."

"The Flatlanders?" said the Chairman.

"Yep," said Farkas. "That's what they call the city dwellers."

Himach and the young men were itching for a change, and the idea of the Flatlanders seemed much more fun than the boring back hills of Waldmeer.

"We do not compromise our high standards under threat or bribery," said the Chairman, pulling himself tall.

He knew that this group of Clinkers were the drug takers and, sometimes, dealers. Getting rid of them would be a great advantage to the town.

"But I suppose the Council would be willing to reconsider its decision under unforeseen circumstances," he added.

Farkas turned to Himach and said, "It's enough. Let's go."

AFTER A FEW DAYS, Amira got another letter from the Council saying they had reconsidered their decision because the complaining parties had withdrawn their objection. She was now free to practice as a healer. Amira didn't know why, but was grateful for the unexpected turnaround. In the afternoon, she walked to Ide's house and showed her the new letter. Ide was also surprised and equally glad.

"I can't believe that stupid Council came to their senses," said Ide to Farkas that evening. "Wonders never cease."

"People who make mistakes are not all bad," said Farkas mysteriously. "Everyone is learning something."

He turned towards his bungalow, leaving Ide to stare after him.

BEGINNINGS
AND ENDINGS

CHAPTER 20
BOOKSHOP

Amira was a frequent visitor to the quaint Waldmeer bookshop. She would scan the shelves to see what people were writing and reading, then sit on the old upholstered chair in the corner with anything that interested her. As she rarely bought any books, she tried to think of another way to repay the owner, Teresa, who had recently taken over the shop.

Teresa was originally a local of Waldmeer, but she had been living in the city for many years. She left Waldmeer when she married a wealthy businessman. Amira thought that money and Teresa were not an obvious match. Although she had a wardrobe full of *rich clothes,* she preferred to wear the ones she got from the op shop. At forty, she still wore her long brown hair in plaits tied with strips of leather. The vintage clothes and the long braids made her look like a bohemian, which she probably was. Her family were farmers, and they were in no way remarkable. Everyone was surprised when she initially attracted Arthur's attention, her future husband. Twenty years older than Teresa, he was sophisticated and worldly-wise. If it had not been for Arthur's mid-life crisis and a conscientious effort at finding a meaningful path, neither would have ever come into contact with the other.

After professional success and marital failures, Arthur decided that a move to the country would help him find a new direction in life. He bought a house in Waldmeer and ran his business from there, with frequent visits to the city and abroad. A sharp intellect meant that Arthur read every trailblazing book that might help him with his mission. He was a regular customer of the bookshop and their biggest buyer. The bookshop was where Arthur and Teresa first met. Initially, Teresa was intimidated by him. However, she was also intrigued. She was certainly flattered by his interest. Arthur soon realised that Teresa had a good heart and a bright mind. She was young and, unlike Arthur, had little baggage from life. He decided that together, they could start from scratch and create the family life he longed for. Thus, the beginning of their fifteen-year journey.

CHAPTER 21
MORE OR LESS

"Do you remember the old bookshop?" said Teresa one morning as Amira browsed the biographies.

"Yes, sure," said Amira. "This bookshop has been here as long as I can remember."

Amira pointed in a complimentary fashion to Teresa's new decor and said, "It didn't look like this."

"From about twelve, I would come here on my way home from school," said Teresa. "My parents didn't have money, but even if they did, I don't think they would have seen the value of spending it on books. In all the years I came here as a schoolgirl, I only ever bought one book, and that was because of Mr MacArthur. When he was the new principal at school, he gave me an award. It was a book voucher. I think the bookshop manager told him about my many visits, and Mr MacArthur probably invented the award so he could give it to me. I used to tell myself that, one day, I would have enough money to buy hundreds of books."

"Little did you realise," said Amira, "that it wasn't that far in your future and you would have not only enough money for any book you wanted but also anything else you wanted."

"I wasn't overly interested in Arthur's money," said Teresa. "I felt that too much money was alienating."

She watched an elderly couple waiting at the bus stop. She enjoyed ordinary people.

"Our relationship wasn't a passionate love affair," continued Teresa. "It was more of a love affair with his books."

She hugged some of the books on her counter in mock dramatic fashion.

"The first time I visited Arthur's house and walked into his hallway, I was in awe. Rows and rows of beautiful books lined every wall. They represented a new world to me, and I was willing to work with whatever that meant in terms of the relationship."

Two customers walked in, and Teresa turned to serve them.

"Before I left Waldmeer," said Teresa when the shop was empty again, "my aunt said to me, 'It is generally not first-generation rich people who have *the problem*. They can usually remember where they came from. It's the second generation.' She didn't say what *the problem* was exactly, but spoilt, delusional, and obnoxious sprang to mind."

Amira smiled. "Yes, they can be the problems of poor little rich kids, but your kids have none of that."

"The money brought me experiences that otherwise would have been totally inaccessible," said Teresa. "And it educated me about many things. Having had it, I now know it is unnecessary to feel less than anyone with money or power. And God help me if I ever think anyone is less than me." She paused. "In the beginning, Arthur was very sincere about his newfound path in life. But it was not maintainable for more than a year or so. It was a rather long, drawn-out, and lonely demise. For sure, the marriage gave its blessings, but it was more of a blessing when it was over."

"You have two beautiful daughters," said Amira warmly. "They are happy here at the school, and you have work that you love. You are still young. You will have another relationship."

"Oh God no," said Teresa emphatically. "I only have enough energy for my kids and my work."

"Perhaps," said Amira, "but men have something to offer that children and work do not."

"I'm not interested in *that*," said Teresa.

"I don't mean 'that' particularly," said Amira as if to entice Teresa back from the land of the renunciate. "Although 'that' is great if things work out that way."

"What then?" asked Teresa.

"Connection. Love," said Amira. "It's a different love to children and work. It will infuriate you, make you cry, make you afraid, and challenge you in every way."

"You are not doing a very good job of selling it," laughed Teresa.

"I don't need to," said Amira. "You already know its worth."

Amira walked towards the door and said, "Next time I come, I'd love to hear what has come your way."

She said it as if it would now be so. Teresa was unsure whether she wanted it, even if it did come her way. Yet, something about the whole conversation seemed to have its own life force.

CHAPTER 22
PRIZE

A few days later, Amira saw Thomas MacArthur in the supermarket.

"Have you been into the bookshop since Teresa has taken it over?" asked Amira.

"No, not yet," said Thomas. "I heard it is looking great. I often see her girls at school, but I haven't caught up with Teresa since her return to Waldmeer. How has she been getting along since her divorce?"

"She's going well," said Amira. "She told me about when you gave her a book voucher as a prize."

"I can't remember that," said Thomas, "because I have probably given ten thousand prizes by now."

He didn't want to count how many years he had been at Waldmeer Secondary School, let alone how many prizes he had given.

"Teresa was a thinker with a lot of potential," said Thomas, "even though there was never much culture in her home. Not to discredit her family, but that's just how it was."

"Why don't you call in and look at the shop?" said Amira.

"I will," said Thomas.

CHAPTER 23
A LITTLE PRAYER

Amira didn't return to the bookshop for a few weeks. When she did, it was crowded with tourists. No one was in the upholstered chair, so she sat with a book. Time must have passed because the shop was empty when she next looked up, and Teresa was looking at her from the counter.

"What's been happening?" asked Amira expectantly.

"Mr MacArthur," said Teresa, "Err, I mean, Thomas has been in quite a few times, and a few days ago, he asked me on a date."

"What did you say?"

"I said 'yes' because you can't say 'no' to the Principal," laughed Teresa. "Seriously, though, after he came in a few times, I realised how much I enjoyed talking to him. He's an attentive listener and kind to my kids at school. I probably need a friend."

As soon as Thomas saw Teresa in the bookshop, he was interested in her. After a few more visits, he was plotting in the harmless way a man like him plots. Normally, Thomas never thought about his ex-students as potential dates or girlfriends. However, in the case of Teresa, he knew that her ex-husband was the same age as him, so he thought it might be a possibility. She was the first woman he had been interested in since Kathleen left.

"That's terrific," said Amira, picking up her shopping bags.

She felt it was an answer to her little prayer for Teresa.

"Something else unexpected also happened," said Teresa.

"What?" asked Amira, putting her bags down again.

"I often go out to see my parents on the farm. As they are now elderly, I need to help a bit," said Teresa. "My dad has employed the young guy from next door's farm. His parents are younger than mine, but they have been there just as long. I remember the guy from when he was a boy. When I left, he was fifteen—awkward, skinny, shy, and, you know, a country boy trying to grow up as best as he could."

"Yes," said Amira, encouraging Teresa to continue.

"He's no shy, skinny, awkward boy anymore!" laughed Teresa.

"Oh, I see," said Amira, laughing as well.

"I have been working with him on the farm jobs whenever I am there and...."

"You like him," said Amira, happy to provide the words.

"Yes," said Teresa. "Do you think that's a bad idea? I mean, he's only thirty. I am hardly one to care about age. I think that's obvious. But do you think I am being silly, setting myself up for something bad to happen?"

"What do you like about him?" asked Amira. "Besides his young, good-looking body."

"I enjoy working with him. He's funny," said Teresa. "We laugh a lot. I haven't laughed that much for ages. He's just glad to be alive. Mostly, it's that *he* seems to like *me*. That means a lot, doesn't it? If the person wants us in their life."

"It's probably the most important thing," said Amira. "Or, at least, the first thing. What is his name?"

"Bryan with a *y*, not an *i*," said Teresa. "I remember his mother saying when he was a baby that she wanted him to have a more exotic name than the family name of Brian. So, Bryan, it became. That's about the extent of his exoticness, I think."

After a pause, Amira reassessed the situation and continued, "Well, that's a surprise. You have gone from no one to two interested parties. And you like them both."

"Yes, for different reasons, I do," said Teresa. "I'm not sure what to do about that."

"Be honest to both," said Amira. "And see where that leads."

CHAPTER 24
GROWING UP

The following weekend, Amira made sure to visit the bookshop. It was as interesting as a good movie. Besides, she felt she couldn't abandon what she had helped create.

Our thoughts and prayers have so much power, thought Amira. *If people realised this, they would be much more careful where they let their thoughts drift.*

"As you suggested, I decided that honesty was the best approach," said Teresa. "In essence, Thomas said 'yes,' and Bryan had a fit and stormed off saying, 'I don't share.'"

"I see," said Amira. "So, you are left with one man standing."

"I don't know," said Teresa screwing up her nose. "If Thomas so easily agrees to something he probably doesn't want, what else does he say 'yes' to when he wants to say 'no'?"

"True," said Amira.

"And Bryan is only thirty. Men don't grow up till they are forty," said Teresa.

"I wouldn't go around saying that to your male friends,"

laughed Amira. "But young men are not very patient and tend to be highly jealous."

"I don't think Bryan is done yet," said Teresa. "At least, I hope not. Otherwise, he would have given up very easily."

Teresa looked bothered, and Amira wanted her to know everything was fine.

"Don't worry," said Amira. "Both relationships, whatever form they may take, now and in the future, are already in motion. They are already bringing up the right issues. Regardless of their outcome, they are working in that good-bad, pleasurable-painful way that important relationships do. Keep your eyes on the straight course of love and trust, and it will help move everything in that direction."

UNFINISHED BUSINESS

CHAPTER 25
CAPTIVATED

Thomas was driving to the city for a meeting with fellow principals. However, he also had another meeting, which was of more importance to him. He had arranged to meet Kathleen at a riverside restaurant near her home. It's not that he wasn't interested in Teresa anymore, but he had called into the bookshop a few days ago with an unexpected request.

"Teresa, I know I have arranged to go out with you next week," said Thomas, "but I was wondering if you would mind postponing it for the time being? I have some unfinished business to attend to in the city."

"Of course, whatever suits you," said Teresa, who was rather surprised.

Until now, everything had been heavily weighted by Thomas's obvious interest in her and her yet-to-be-convinced response.

Well, there you go, thought Teresa when Thomas had gone. *Life is full of surprises.*

As Thomas drove along the country bends, he didn't turn the radio on. Instead, he reflected on the course of his recent thoughts, which had become increasingly focused on Teresa. After discovering that he had a rival in young Bryan, he often found himself lost in plotting how to win Teresa over. However, one morning as he sat on his balcony watching the rosellas with their early tasks, age and wisdom finally had a moment to speak.

"Haven't you noticed how stressed you are?" said Thomas's inner voice.

"Now that you mention it," said Thomas, "I am getting myself in a state."

"And have you noticed," said the voice, "that your physical health has deteriorated lately?"

"Yes," said Thomas, "my energy levels have been diminishing, and I don't feel that well. I don't want to get ill."

"Do you have any idea what the problem might be?" said the voice.

Thomas was about to say *no* when he decided to ask the question properly and listen for a proper answer. Suddenly, as if someone had opened the curtain, he could see the problem.

"Oh, I see," said Thomas. "I am running away, aren't I? I have given up on trying to heal anything with Kathleen and have made myself busy with a new story, imagining it might be less painful and more rewarding."

"Yes," said the voice, "you told yourself that Teresa is a better story. Since its inception, you have not thought about why your relationship with Kathleen broke down and if those same reasons might affect any future relationship."

If Thomas was honest with himself, which he currently was, all he had been thinking about was how to convince Teresa that he was better for her than Bryan. The underlying premise was that if he could win Teresa, he would be happy. He had become a mental captive, although he was not entirely sure who the captor was. Teresa hadn't forced him to think that way. Regardless, he had lost his peace of mind. In retrospect, it all seemed a little embarrassing. It wasn't that the idea of Teresa was foolish, but how he had so easily let his imaginings grow unchecked.

What was I thinking it was going to give me? After all this time, am I so easily fooled? thought Thomas with uneasy humility.

Perhaps it was shame more than humility. Either would do for now. The voice was gone, having done its job.

CHAPTER 26
COOLING OFF

In Eraldus:

Two months had passed since Amira had last seen or spoken to Gabriel. She felt that, as he was a newlywed, she should leave him alone.

We should respect other people's decisions, thought Amira, *even if they seem bad to us. Perhaps we are wrong. Perhaps we are not wrong, but the decision is necessary for the person's growth.*

While Thomas was driving from Waldmeer to the city to see Kathleen, Amira walked to her local cafe in Eraldus and ran into Gabriel.

"Hi," said Amira.

Gabriel smiled, but it was a little forced. Amira wondered if he didn't want to be friends anymore. She sat in her usual spot in the cafe and put her head in the paper as he went to the counter for takeaway. After a few minutes, he came over and sat down. Both were trying to salvage what had so quickly become a fragile relationship.

That which holds us all together, thought Amira, *is very delicate.*

"How are you?" asked Gabriel.

"I'm fine. And you?" said Amira, sounding a little more formal than she could help.

"Yep, great, thanks," said Gabriel.

Amira looked down. She didn't want to have a meaningless conversation. Gabriel looked at the door and seemed to be making an important decision. He visibly braced himself.

"I'm not going that well," he said as if the words had defeated him. "I'm sorry I haven't been in contact, but I've been busy."

"It's alright," said Amira. "You have work, and now you also have Paul to consider."

Thinking it might be best to ask a few questions, she said, "What have you decided to do about the share house? Only you and Paul are there now. Charlie and Mary have bought their own place and..."

She stopped short of saying, *You and Paul share the same bedroom, so you have two empty bedrooms.*

"Paul and I are still in our own rooms," said Gabriel. "I told him that I like my own space."

"We don't have to be on top of each other all the time," said Amira.

She then realised that her phrase "on top of each other" was conjuring up an image for both of them, but the words had already come out.

"Yeah, we are on top of each other," said Gabriel.

In fact, the bedroom issue was a spiky one for him and Paul and had caused numerous arguments.

"We've been looking at houses to buy and signed a contract last week," said Gabriel.

"Wow," said Amira. "Congratulations."

"Yesterday was the last day of the cooling-off period," said Gabriel. "I told Paul I couldn't go through with the contract, so we withdrew our offer."

After signing the buyer's contract of sale, Gabriel woke up in a cold sweat every morning. Finally, he realised that, for whatever reason, he couldn't go through with it. Amira thought that buying a house and committing to a big mortgage with Paul had had more of an effect on Gabriel than marrying him.

"I can't buy a house with Paul," said Gabriel, grabbing his coffee and standing up to leave, "because... because I can't."

Amira sat there on her own for some time.

It is the ongoing interplay between independence and intimacy, she thought. *Push too far into independence, and we disconnect and hurt each other. Push too far into intimacy, and we get afraid of losing ourselves in it. So, we head the other way. Thus, the cycle perpetuates itself.*

A customer broke her train of thought, "Excuse me, Miss. I notice you aren't reading your paper. Would you mind if I took it?"

"Of course," said Amira, who realised she had been hogging one of the two free cafe papers.

As she passed it to him, he smiled and said, "What a lovely morning. I hope you have a beautiful day."

He was a cheery fellow, full of joie de vivre.

"And you too," said Amira.

CHAPTER 27
GAROURINN

In Waldmeer:

Amira rarely spoke about her personal life. Whenever people asked about her life, she said something carefully appropriate. However, Ide was a good soul, self-assured enough not to be jealous of other people's happiness or happy at other people's misery. When Amira next saw her, she confided in her about Gabriel.

"You know how Gabriel got married and hasn't been to Waldmeer since?" said Amira.

"Yes?" replied Ide.

"I saw him in Eraldus during the week," said Amira.

"How is he going?" asked Ide.

"I have a feeling that things are not going well with Paul," said Amira.

"Oh, that's a shame," said Ide. "Perhaps, they will work it out. Lots of couples have problems adjusting to each other in the beginning."

"Perhaps," said Amira.

She kissed Ide on the cheek and said, "Goodbye, love. I'll see you later."

That afternoon, Ide knocked on the bungalow door. Normally, she didn't go to the bungalow. She always let Farkas come to her if he wanted anything.

"I saw Amira at the shops," said Ide, "and she told me that Gabriel and Paul aren't doing very well."

"Of course, they aren't," said Farkas abruptly.

"What do you mean, of course?" asked Ide.

She was confused why Farkas would assume to know such a thing.

"How do you know?" she repeated.

Farkas wouldn't reply and looked angry. Ide was startled. Farkas was never angry with her. She never gave him any reason to be.

The next morning, when it was still dark, Farkas made his bed, gathered his things together, ensured the bungalow was neat, and closed the door. He quietly opened Ide's back door, which he knew was always unlocked, and left a note on the kitchen table.

> I am going away for a little while.
> I left money on the bed.
> If I am gone longer than what the money covers, rent out the bungalow to someone else.
> Farkas

He knew Ide would be upset, and Christopher too. However, he had unfinished business to attend to. He hadn't slept much last night. Finally, at 3.00 a.m., he knew what to do. Go to the Leleks, cross Erdo's old walking bridge, head for the North Country, and visit the wolf pack. The last time he had seen them was three winters ago. It was summer now, so that the weather wouldn't be a problem.

Farkas reached the bridge and felt Erdo's eyes on him, but he did not see him. He wondered if he would remember the way, but as with all those who travel to the North Country, it is not the terrain that gets them there but the state of mind.

Over a few days, the rhythmic nature of uninterrupted walking settled his mind, and he found himself at the North Country pass. Somewhere along the pass, the wolves would meet him. That was what happened last time. He was confident of finding them. He got to the end of the pass, and strangely, he had not seen or felt the slightest inkling of them. As he sat under the shade of a large over-hanging rock, he recalled that last time he also sat under a similar ledge in the middle of a ferocious storm, and the Head Gardener of Garourinn appeared and saved him.

"You are wise to call me again," said the familiar voice.

Farkas turned towards the Head Gardener. He was not sure that he *had* called him.

"This time, you will not be with the wolf pack," said the Head Gardener. "Go straight ahead to Garourinn."

With that, he left. Having come so far, Farkas decided to keep walking. After about an hour, his old friend, Milyaket, from the Homeland, appeared by his side. Farkas was very fond of Milyaket. However, she was so ethereal that he mostly had no idea how to relate to her.

"Have you had a good journey?" said Milyaket.

Farkas always behaved around her.

"Yes, thank you," he said.

"I will escort you to Garourinn. The Master wishes to see you," said Milyaket.

"The Master?" asked Farkas.

"There is one above the Head Gardener," said Milyaket. "We call him the Master because he is."

CHAPTER 28

MASTER

n the Garden of Garourinn (inter-dimensional):

They soon passed through the gates of Garourinn. Farkas looked at the sweet cottages mixed amongst the green fields, but sensed they were not for him.

"You will be sleeping in the Master's house," said Milyaket.

Over the hill was a large but unpretentious group of buildings. On entering one of the buildings, Milyaket showed Farkas his room on the second floor.

"The Master will see you when it is time," said Milyaket.

Farkas ate with the other residents and was given various tasks in the house, along with everyone else. The other residents were rather monk-like, with simple clothes and gentle demeanours. They were slightly aloof from him as if it was not their place to engage with him too fully, although they were always pleasant.

The days glided by. Farkas wasn't unhappy to be there. It wasn't exciting, but it wasn't boring. Time was marked by meals, domestic tasks, being in the gardens, and exploring the many different buildings. Next door was an extensive library. As there was no other form of entertainment, Farkas occasionally went to the library and picked up random books. The books were not like ordinary books. They were alive with distinct personalities.

He often passed the prayer hall, which the residents attended several times a day. The stillness from the large hall was so powerful that it seemed somewhat disconcerting to Farkas. One evening, he walked past the prayer hall and heard the unfamiliar sound of crying. Peeking through the door, he saw that one of the monks was distressed. The rest of the monks moved to surround him. Some held hands. Others lifted their hands skywards. Others stood motionless. Little bits of light came from each monk and joined above the distressed monk. The light interweaved and formed a radiant ball of orange and white luminescence. It grew much bigger than the sum of the individual lights from all the monks. The monk stopped crying and sat with a transfixed look on his face. Some of the light reached out a stray arm and touched Farkas lightly. It felt incredibly, deliciously inviting.

It feels so precious, thought Farkas, although *precious* was not a word he would normally use.

As HE WAS ABOUT to go to breakfast the next morning, Milyaket knocked on his door. She always wore flowing gowns, so Farkas never saw her body. He had the impression that she was floating across the floor rather than walking. Her soft green and pink aura made her even more beautiful than usual.

"Today will be your last day with us," said Milyaket.

Farkas hadn't thought about leaving for a while.

"The Master is ready to see you," said Milyaket. "I will take you to him."

They went into a part of the building that he had never noticed. Milyaket stopped at a heavy, dark door and bowed to Farkas.

"Until we meet again," she said.

The door had no handle or lock. Farkas was about to ask how to open it, but it opened of its own accord. When he entered the room, he felt all his movements were magnified. He tried to breathe quietly and walk even more quietly, but he felt like an elephant.

"Sit next to me," said a commanding but kind voice in the corner.

As Farkas's eyes adjusted to the light, he saw a man, perhaps forty years old, sitting on a lounge and looking out over the surrounding mountains. Although Farkas felt he should be nervous at meeting the Master, he felt relaxed. Not relaxed like when we let ourselves deteriorate into lethargy, but relaxed like when we feel loved without having to do anything or be anything.

"You have an unanswered question?" said the Master.

"Yes," said Farkas. "When I was with the wolf pack in the North Country, its leader, Galahad, told me that Maria was my sister under a different name."

He wondered if the issue needed more explanation and added, "Maria now calls herself Amira."

He then felt embarrassed at telling the Master something he, no doubt, already knew.

"You and Amira have shared a number of lives," said the Master. "Some have been on Earth, and some have been else-where. More than once, she was your sister and more than once, she was your partner. Whenever she was your sister, things tended to go well. Whenever she was your partner, it ended badly or sadly."

Farkas did not feel better for the information.

"The problem is not whether you have a sister or love relation-ship," continued the Master without judgment. "The problem is your concept of love. It must be outgrown or, if you prefer, refined.

It is my task to help you with this. However, it is a collaborative venture. I cannot help you if you do not allow it."

The Master softly drew his hand over Farkas's hair as if he were bonding with a young child and led him to the door, which opened automatically.

"Love is to free, not to imprison," said the Master.

Usually, those were words Farkas wouldn't entertain for a passing moment, but now they were embedded in his mind. That's what happens when the Master speaks.

In Waldmeer:

Ide heard a commotion outside. Christopher was calling out excitedly.

"He's back, Mum," yelled Christopher, who was still young enough to blurt out what he really wanted to say uncensored.

Thank God, thought Ide.

She saw Farkas and Christopher walking down to the bungalow, laughing and joking.

"We have some leftover dinner if you want Christopher to get you some," she said.

"Thanks," said Farkas, pushing Christopher towards his mother. "Go get the plate from your mother. And do the washing up for her, too."

He walked into the bungalow and said to himself, *One step at a time.*

COUPLE

CHAPTER 29
HALF-HALF

In Waldmeer:

Ide had spent the last two days trying to make a workable budget. It still wasn't working. Adding to the problem was her difficulty getting full-time work at Waldmeer Hospital. She was an excellent nurse, and the patients often specifically asked for her. She treated everyone with the same care she would with her own relatives. However, the Matron had been at the hospital almost as long as it had been there, or so it seemed. She held onto the full-time positions for the locals. Ide wasn't born in Waldmeer, so Matron did not have her on the *special* list. Besides, the Matron was more than a little jealous of Ide. Not only did the patients love Ide, but it did not go unnoticed that Ide's patients seemed to heal faster and have fewer complications than most other patients. Ide was, after all, a descendant of the Clinkers, and they have healing in them. Matron didn't know about Ide's connection with the Clinkers, and Ide certainly wasn't telling her. It would have given Matron more ammunition, and she already had enough. There seemed to be only one sensible solution.

"I'm going to have to sell the house," Ide said to Farkas. "The mortgage is impossible for me."

Farkas didn't reply. He could see by the expression on her face that she was both serious and upset. At the end of that week, Farkas brought the topic up again.

"That bungalow is too small for me," he said as if Ide had only just mentioned selling the house. "I've had enough of living in it."

"Yes, I understand. You need a proper place," said Ide with resignation.

"I've found one," said Farkas.

"Really?" said Ide, trying to sound cheery but feeling she was losing him faster than anticipated.

"There is an old guy not far from here who is recently widowed," said Farkas. "He hates living in the house without his wife. He wants a quick sale so that he can move to his son's family."

"You are thinking of buying, not renting?" said Ide.

"I have the money," said Farkas. "I don't want to keep renting. The house is fairly rundown. That and the fact that the guy wants a quick sale means it is a good price."

"That's wonderful," said Ide. "You will love having your own home again."

"I haven't finished," said Farkas with mock sternness. "I have the money, but don't want to put that much money into a house again. Also, it has three bedrooms. Too big for me. I don't want to rent the rooms out. You know I can't tolerate people."

"Yes," agreed Ide, knowing that was all too true and wondering where he was leading.

"So," said Farkas, "I thought you might be interested in jointly buying the house with me, half and half. That way, you would at least own half a house for you and Christopher."

Ide sat there dumbfounded.

"You're not that young anymore," Farkas continued with a half-smile. "You have to consider your financial future."

Ide didn't want to make it seem too big a deal in case it made Farkas feel awkward.

"You and I jointly own it?" she queried to make sure she had not misheard him.

"Yes," said Farkas.

"And if, for some reason, it didn't quite work after a while?" asked Ide.

"Then one of us could buy the other out, or we'd sell it," said Farkas.

This was a considerable risk for both of them. Would Farkas be able to tolerate living with Ide and Christopher in the same house? Would Ide be able to tolerate Farkas? In such close proximity, would their relationship fall apart? Could they trust each other financially? And probably most dangerous, what sort of relationship were they getting into? Friends don't jointly own homes. Lovers do, but they were not lovers. She couldn't ask him for clarification. Even if she did, she didn't think he would have an answer. There were, undoubtedly, many more glaring risks than positives. Ide glanced out the window to break the stream of warnings. She remembered her husband, Fabian, who was now in the Homeland. Did she regret the risks she took with Fabian despite all the problems? No. Ide became still, and a cloak of calm seemed to float onto her shoulders. Perhaps it was Fabian.

She turned back to Farkas and said steadily, "I heard today at work that we are getting a new hospital administrator. He is known for modernising everything and removing the old pecking order. There is a good chance that I will be able to get a full-time, permanent position at the hospital. If I do, it would be a great time to buy half a house."

That was all Farkas wanted and needed. He stood up, looking pleased and relieved.

"I'll ring the agent to see when we can look at it," he said.

The following week, they signed the contract. As they walked out of the real estate office, Farkas reached over and kissed Ide on the cheek. He had never touched her, let alone kissed her.

Ide said too quietly for him to hear, but perhaps he did, "God help us both."

CHAPTER 30
SOFT BELLY

Teresa ran her hand slowly down Bryan's back. It was brown and strong. When she reached the small of his back and onto his backside, it changed to white but was just as defined. She smiled at the whiteness of the skin not exposed to long days outside on the farm. He was still waking up.

"Now that Thomas has dumped you, I suppose you have no choice but me," joked Bryan.

"He didn't exactly dump me," protested Teresa.

"I'd say he did," said Bryan. "You were seeing him. He stopped seeing you. In my books, that's dumping."

"Oh, okay," smiled Teresa.

She had heard that Thomas had reconnected with his ex-girl-friend, Kathleen. She was glad for him and hoped it worked out. Bryan reached for Teresa and then poked her soft belly.

"Hey, I have had two children," said Teresa defensively.

She thought she heard Bryan saying that he liked it soft, but she wasn't sure because his words were muffled by his kissing her belly.

Not surprisingly, Teresa and her ex-husband, Arthur, never

had much of a sexual relationship. They were not drawn together that way, and it did not bloom as the years passed. The little sexual contact they had in the earlier years shrivelled into virtually nothing. Until Bryan, Teresa had not experienced a vibrant and close sexual relationship. It was a considerable part of what attracted them, how they bonded, and the enjoyment they derived from each other. They were falling in love with each other's bodies as much as with each other.

Teresa's girls were in the city for the weekend with their father. They didn't know about Bryan. Teresa felt that, at this stage, they didn't need to know. Besides, if they knew, Arthur would also know, and he had a vindictive side. Bryan was no match for someone like Arthur. Arthur was unlikely to find happiness in another relationship due to his unwillingness to learn, so he would likely be vengeful. Teresa knew her enemy and was well prepared to protect her new life and her new love.

However, she had another enemy she was not so well-equipped to fight—Bryan's mother, Clarice. Bryan was the apple of his mother's eye, and she had plans for him. Being involved with an older woman was not one of them. Clarice could hardly manipulate a forty-year-old woman with Teresa's life experience. Teresa made sure to point out to Bryan that Clarice was not her mother and that he must cope with her himself. What made matters worse was that he still lived at home out of the convenience of working on the family farm. It did cross Teresa's mind that Bryan may be too young for her and not mature enough to deal with his mother, but then she would look into his open, transparent, blue eyes and remember that this was his journey as much as hers. They may be learning different things, but they were learning them together. It was enough to know that.

CHAPTER 31
NEED OR LOVE

In the city:

"This is delicious," said Gabriel.

"I knew you'd like it," said Paul. "You always do."

As Gabriel was about to take his dinner plate to the sink, Paul stopped him.

"Sit down for a while," said Paul.

"I've got heaps of work to do tonight. Can we talk later?" asked Gabriel.

"It's important," said Paul.

Gabriel sat down again. The thought crossed his mind that he hadn't looked closely at Paul for a while. Paul looked sad.

"What's the matter?" asked Gabriel.

"This is hard for me to say," said Paul with a quiver. "You see, I love you."

"Of course you do," said Gabriel. "And I love you."

"That's the thing, right there," said Paul. "Do you?"

Gabriel went to speak, but Paul put his hand up.

"I don't want to fight about this," said Paul. "It's too important. Ever since we met, I have loved you. You are, for me, the perfect mate—handsome, creative, kind, and funny. I couldn't have been more thrilled when you took an interest in me. At the bottom of my heart, I always knew that you didn't quite feel the same way about me as I do about you, but I was willing to take whatever you wanted to give me. Besides, I have lived in the hope of getting you to love me more. I don't think you realise how much it hurts when you pull away from me. It's not just about not buying the house. You do it in a thousand different ways. I tell myself that you are entitled to your independence. If I want to be with you, I have to accept that you need a lot of it. Sometimes, I feel embarrassed when other people think you don't love me. It's humiliating."

Paul stood up, went and got tissues, and wiped his eyes.

"I suppose," said Paul, "to be fair, maybe it is need more than love. I say how much I love you. Perhaps, a great deal of it is need. I feel so much better with you in my life, and I am terrified of losing you. Today, I told myself that trying to get you to love me will never make you love me. That breaks my heart."

Paul nodded to indicate that he was done.

"I don't want to say anything lightly," said Gabriel, "because what you have said deserves a proper response. Let me think about it."

He hugged Paul, and both could not help but feel the other's soul intertwine. Paul felt exhausted and went to bed.

Gabriel watched him and thought, *So much of what he said is probably true. I do push him away, but I can't stand neediness. I would rather be single than feel trapped. But maybe it's more than that.*

Paul rolled over and went into a deep sleep.

CHAPTER 32
LITTLE BOOK OF HEALING

T homas hadn't seen Kathleen all year. He walked up the steps of the riverside restaurant, telling himself to be calm and breathe. He need not have worried. There was no denying their relationship ended with a rift, but Kathleen was not the sort of woman to hold onto such things. Besides, there was still a lot of love between them. They sat outside on the verandah to enjoy the glorious day. There was much to catch up on. They never had a problem talking to each other. Kathleen reached into her bag. Thomas recognised a familiar green cover.

"Are you reading *The Little Book of Healing*?" asked Thomas. "I have been studying the lessons in it all year. I got it from Amira."

"What a coincidence," said Kathleen. "So have I. My brother, Aishi, gave it to me at the beginning of the year. He has lots of fantastic books at the retreat centre. It has been travelling everywhere with me in my handbag."

"Me too," said Thomas. "Not in my handbag."

His laughter helped him to relax. The thought of them independently choosing to study the same book gave him courage.

Perhaps, he thought, *we are not as disconnected as I believed.*

"Kathleen," he said, "we need to talk about what happened. I'm not asking you to come back to me, but we are too old to let a good relationship die without giving it every chance to survive. I don't care in what way it survives." He shuffled and lowered his eyes. "Survive, that's all. Not die completely."

Thomas's directness gave Kathleen a little hope that it was worth the emotional effort to talk about it.

"Let's not have a blame talk," she said. "That would only make things worse. However, I do believe that we must be honest with each other. The pain caused in the situation warrants an honest attempt to address it, don't you think?"

"Yes, I do," said Thomas.

"I also don't want to talk about the details of what happened," said Kathleen, "or I am afraid we will get nowhere."

"Agreed," said Thomas.

"For me, the bottom line is that I feel I can't trust you," said Kathleen. "That may come as a surprise because you probably see yourself as a very trustworthy person. In many ways, you are. But in others, you are not."

"I think that is harsh," said Thomas.

"Perhaps," said Kathleen, "but you are asking for my trust, and I don't give it lightly. I must know that the person I am trusting is trustworthy. Otherwise, you will betray me in a thousand small ways, if not big ones."

"I won't try to defend myself," said Thomas. "I can't see myself being that way. However, I trust you are saying this in good will to help us both."

"Yes, that is all I am asking," said Kathleen. "To look at it. To try. If I feel you are trying, then I will be satisfied."

Kathleen said that she would like to go home.

As they hugged goodbye, she asked, "By the way, what lesson are you up to in the book?"

Thomas replied, "The one that says, *We can learn to use the pain in our relationships to transform us, turning them into entities that heal, not harm.*"

"That was my lesson last week," said Kathleen. "We are not too far apart."

PETALS AND SWEET PEAS

CHAPTER 33
ENOUGH

In Waldmeer:

Amira and Ide were sitting at Ide's kitchen table in her new house.

"Sorry, it's still such a mess," said Ide.

"Not at all," said Amira. "It's coming along really well. I must tell you that you have inspired me with a big change. After you explained your budget and how the new house came about, I started to think about my situation. I am very grateful to have inherited not one but two lovely little homes. I doubt I would ever have been able to buy a home myself. However, I thought about how much travel I do back and forth to Eraldus each week. Also, how expensive it is to run two homes and the maintenance. If I only had one home, I could use the money from the other to help as an income. I don't make much money from either of my practices. I always seem to end up doing much of it for free. But I have been given so much, why would I complain? I asked myself if I were only to have one house, which one would I choose? Waldmeer won, hands down. Besides, the Eraldus house is worth much more than the Waldmeer one. It's the land value. So, I will put it up for sale this week."

"What about your city clients?" asked Ide.

"I'm not sure," said Amira. "They can ring me. I will start writing newsletters for them. I don't know how it will work, but life changes. We often have to go with the flow, not knowing its course. Things can change because there is something better or different for us. If we don't follow our leanings, that which once seemed fine will start to feel unsatisfactory and will dismantle because it is not right for us anymore. It becomes a burden rather than the blessing it once was. We must trust that, as we were cared for in the past, we will be cared for in the future."

"It will make your life simpler," said Ide.

"My Great-Aunt Rose would say, 'Enough is ample sufficiency.' One house is enough. And Waldmeer is enough," said Amira.

After a moment, she added, "It's very quiet. Christopher is at school, but where is Farkas?"

"Who knows?" said Ide. "I never ask. I want this to work."

She pointed to the house. But, perhaps, she was pointing to something more than the house. Amira nodded sympathetically.

"I told him you were coming this morning," said Ide.

"What did he say?" asked Amira.

"Nothing," said Ide. "When he left earlier, I asked if he wanted to stay and see you. He said, 'No, you have no idea how annoying she can be. And offensive.'"

Amira laughed.

"You're not offended, are you?" said Ide. "Otherwise, I wouldn't have told you."

"No, of course not," said Amira. "It's true. But I do pick my people. Or, at least, someone picks them. I'm only annoying (and possibly offensive) if I think the person can cope. Besides, we have a responsibility to give our best to others. Sometimes, our best is not what people want to hear."

"Yes, but if I did that," said Ide, "we'd be ripping up the house contract within a few weeks."

"Absolutely. You just be yourself," said Amira. "That is what is right, and that is what will work."

CHAPTER 34
SACRED AND WORTHY

As Amira reached her gate, she could see Gabriel's car. She reminded herself that as he was renting the bungalow, it was his to come and go as he pleased, with whomever he pleased. She opened the gate and walked along the curving path to her front door.

Waldmeer had ideal weather for gardens. Plenty of sunshine and rain. That was why the rainforest backing onto Waldmeer was so alive and wondrous. Often, Amira would throw seeds around the garden beds, and then, without another thought, they would grow into beautiful flowers within a month or two. It was the easiest gardening ever. She reached down to pick some of the sweet peas bordering the path. They were climbing everywhere, up the roses and over the lavender.

I'll get some of each colour—pink, mauve, red, and white, she thought.

"You don't have any yellow ones," said a voice.

Amira looked up. It was Gabriel. He picked some yellow ones and passed them to her.

"Thank you," said Amira.

"Where have you been this morning?" asked Gabriel.

"I was visiting Ide and Farkas's new house," said Amira.

"Do they have a house together?" asked Gabriel.

"Yes," said Amira.

Gabriel looked confused but shrugged and said, "What's it like?"

"It needs a lot of fixing up, but it will be lovely when done."

Amira stood up and brushed the garden dirt off her clothes.

"Farkas told Ide that I'm annoying and offensive," she said.

Gabriel turned for his car and said over his shoulder, "For once, I'd agree with him."

Later that day, Amira crossed paths with Gabriel again.

No sight of Paul yet, thought Amira. *Perhaps he didn't come.*

"Are you on your own, Gabriel?" she ventured.

"Yes," said Gabriel.

"I have made an important decision," said Amira.

"What is it?" asked Gabriel, wondering if it might also affect him.

"I am going to sell my Eraldus home and live here permanently," said Amira.

Gabriel looked at Amira for a few moments. He remembered that he had found their share house when Amira first moved to Eraldus.

My God, that seems like an eternity ago, he thought.

He wasn't sure what Amira's decision meant for him or if it meant anything at all. He told himself that it was her business.

"Whatever you want," he said and continued walking to the bungalow.

Amira returned to her garden. It was a large cottage garden that had been faithfully cared for by her parents since they built the small fibro house decades ago. She no longer tended the vegetable patch. The hen run at the bottom of the garden was now uninhabited by feathered friends who had all died of old age. The orchard thrived with virtually no care. It was well established and reaped the benefit of her father's nurturing for many years. Amira loved the flower beds. She had a knack with flowers. They grew enthusiastically and spread beauty with minimal attention. That is the whole idea of a cottage garden—unlabored, unpretentious, homely, and reassuring.

Walking through the flowers, Amira reflected, *I do not want to annoy or offend anyone. However, to the ego, it can often be seen that way. It is constantly on guard and looking for all the ways it will be betrayed and hurt. If we listen with our fears, then almost everything is a threat. If we listen with our spirit, then no offence is taken. The voice we listen with changes our perception.*

As she had so much travelling to do, the Waldmeer garden had not infrequently been on the brink of chaos, at which point she would spend a few hours fixing it up so it would be manageable again. It had so many plants, bulbs, and seeds that it could run away with itself very quickly. Now that Amira was about to enter a different phase of her life, when she could settle into the routine of one house and one town, she looked at the garden with fresh eyes. She didn't want to tame it. That would be a shame to tame such a thing. Besides, no matter how wild it got, there was always an invisible, underlying, loose order.

Gardens remind us to be patient and humble because that's what they are, thought Amira. *They have no delusions of grandeur or plotting schemes. They trust implicitly that they will be cared for as part of the cycle of nature. They give so much, yet they are unaware of their gift. They have no perception of themselves. They treat all their inhabitants, of every type and form, as sacred and worthy. They surrender themselves to the moment with flawless confidence and the unmarred hope of renewal.*

PART II
TOGETHER IN TIME

ONE YEAR ON

CHAPTER 35
ACCIDENT

One year had passed. There had been a little accident. Perhaps, *accident* was not quite the right word, but *little* was. Farkas was standing by Ide's bed in Waldmeer Hospital. They were both staring adoringly at their brand-new baby boy. Farkas had hoped for a little girl, but regardless, the intensity of his feelings of love for and protectiveness over the child surprised him. Ide had secretly known it was a boy. Her Clinker instinct told her. If that had not told her, the look on the ultrasound technician's face many months ago had given it away. She had worked in hospitals too long not to be able to read the silent language of its professionals. Still, they had agreed to let it be a revelation at birth, so Ide kept it in her heart.

It wasn't exactly a planned birth. The sex was not planned, and the pregnancy was even more not planned. After a few months of sharing the same house, Farkas and Ide occasionally slept together. One would have thought that a woman who already had a child, had been married for a decade, and was working in the nursing profession would have had no miscalculation regarding contraception. However, Ide was by nature unsympathetic to drugs. Her instinct was to keep them out of her system. Of course, she did something else instead. She may have been alternative in her thinking, but she wasn't stupid. She knew everything about natural fertility planning and followed it meticulously. Or, so she thought. Perhaps she did follow it correctly, but this little one was determined to come no matter what she did.

When Ide first discovered she was pregnant, she cried for two days. She was stunned, afraid, and worried about the future. They hardly had a conventional, stable situation at home. Only after the two days, when she had reached a point of peace about it, did she tell Farkas. She didn't want to have to deal with his reaction until she was strong enough. He said nothing for a week. He thought about leaving and told himself he didn't want a child. He wasn't worried about the child's future. He knew that, come rain or shine, Ide would be there for that child. He was worried about his capacity and readiness to be a father. By the week's end, he decided to give it a go. Besides, he told himself that the wheel was already in motion.

"The child is coming whether you stay or leave," said Ide. "My path is already set. I would like you to stay, and the baby would want that too. However, it is your choice. I will not hold it against you if you go."

"I will stay for now," said Farkas. "I'm sorry, but honestly, that's the best I can promise at the moment."

"When you first moved into the bungalow, you said the same," said Ide. "You are still here."

After that, Farkas relaxed and let himself enjoy the whole process. Every time he felt the fear and anxiety come up, he reminded himself that he was not trapped and that everything could even work out well.

CHAPTER 36
BABIES

Amira was returning from a hospital visit to Ide and her new baby. She sat in the corner of the Waldmeer cafe, thought about how adorable the baby was, and watched the Christmas holidaymakers. Her eyes were drawn to a mother and two girls at an outside table. The younger girl grabbed some of her sister's gingerbread man. A squabble ensued. Instead of dealing with it, the mother began to cry and rested her head in her hands. The youngest daughter looked worried and jumped up to pat her head. As the woman wiped her eyes, Amira realised it was Melissa, the mother of the girls she had looked after in Eraldus several years ago. On closer inspection, the fighting girls were indeed Marilyn and Bianca. They would now be eight and seven.

I see my darlings have returned to their naughty ways, thought Amira.

She probably meant Melissa as much as the children. Amira waited until the mother's tears had a chance to dry and then walked outside as if she hadn't seen them.

"Maria!" squealed both the children as Amira hugged them tightly.

Amira stopped working with the family before her Homeland transition and name change. They did not know that she lived in Waldmeer now. They all exchanged news, and the little family brightened up considerably. Melissa sent the girls across the road to the beach and spoke with Amira more earnestly.

"Much has happened in the last six months," said Melissa. "My husband and I have been through a rough patch. He became involved with an American woman who he was working with. He was honest enough to tell me about it, although we kept it from the children. We tried to work things out. We went to counselling, had many arguments, cried a lot, and then he left. He moved to the United States with his new partner, saying he would save money to bring the girls over for regular holidays. It's not just the emotional damage of the whole thing. The girls and I are having real survival issues. These days, my work means I am travelling all over the state. Obviously, that doesn't work with two little girls, and I have no relatives to help me. I have asked for work in the city, but they cannot give it to me for another year. I can't afford to lose this job. In desperation, I told the girls that we would have a few days in Waldmeer. I hoped that an angel would tell me what to do."

"I have an idea," said Amira suddenly. "Why don't I speak with Thomas MacArthur, the high school principal here in Waldmeer? He is a friend. I will ask him if the girls can enrol in the primary school for the year. Every Monday morning early, you could drive from Eraldus and drop them at school on your way to wherever you are going in the country. I will pick them up after school on Monday. They can stay with me for the school week and be picked up again by you after school on Friday."

"I don't know what to say," said Melissa. "I have to accept because I have no alternative. To say the girls will be thrilled is an understatement."

The girls ran wildly back from the beach. Bianca grabbed a piece of Marilyn's hair, and the older sister complained bitterly.

We'll be sorting out that behaviour fairly quickly, Amira thought.

"You tell the girls," said Amira. "I'll go and prepare my two spare bedrooms. Call in on your way home so that they can see where they will be staying."

Looks like I'll be getting my babies back, thought Amira.

CHAPTER 37
ANGEL

Although angels were not something Amira generally saw, there was one that she did occasionally see. She could *see* it just enough to know that it was large (larger than a person), took a masculine form, and (like all angels) was loving and powerful. However, she had not seen this angel for some time because she had not seen its accompanying human. It was Gabriel's angel. The angel only ever said one thing to Amira, which was repeated on several occasions. It was, *Be patient. He doesn't know what he is doing.* He would then look at Gabriel as if there was nothing he could do that could ever break that love. Amira never told Gabriel any of this because he didn't believe in angels, and he would have been offended that the angel thought that one needed patience to deal with him.

Amira hadn't seen Gabriel for the past six months. The six months before that, he occasionally came to Waldmeer and worked in the bungalow. One day, he told Amira that she should rent the bungalow out to someone else because he wasn't there enough. He said she should let him know when it had been arranged, and he would come and take all his things. Amira agreed, but she neither rented it out nor contacted him. He also did nothing, so the bungalow stood there with half-finished artwork and unused bed. The modest, little bungalow had been in the back garden a long time and, before that, had stood on the grounds of the Waldmeer hotel for even longer. It had time on its side.

CHAPTER 38

KAHWAH

Thomas was having one of his biannual styling visits with Gabriel. He would collect Gabriel once he got to Eraldus, drive to the large shopping centre, buy whatever Gabriel deemed worthy, have a coffee and a talk, and then go on to his other meetings in the city. Thomas's day would end with Kathleen over dinner. She always picked the restaurant. To get Thomas out of his comfort zone, she deliberately picked all sorts of weird and wonderful places.

Tonight, it was the *Afghan Light*. It was an endearing and interesting place. Everyone sat on elaborately decorated cushions inside a tent made from heavily embroidered fabrics, drinking tea called Kahwah. The tea was a combination of green tea, cardamom pods, cinnamon bark, saffron strands, ginger, and almonds. Like Masala tea from India and Kashmiri tea from Pakistan, the exact recipe is unique to each family. The first cup of tea was sweetened, and the next was not. Thomas mentioned to Kathleen that it was a bit like love.

"First," said Thomas, "you get pulled in by the loveliness, then you get beaten by the issues."

Kathleen laughed and replied, "Who would willingly walk the path of love without first being seduced by its promise?"

In his own way, Gabriel did a version of the restaurant choosing technique with Thomas's clothes. He would pick clothes for Thomas that were pushing the boundary but not over the line, hoping to modernise his style. He had mixed success. He could usually tell how the last six months had gone as soon as he saw whatever Thomas was wearing. Today, Thomas looked a little better. His pants were outdated, but his shirt was borderline okay. Quite frequently, Gabriel would pick things that looked great in the shop, but as soon as Thomas wore them, they seemed to change into looking different and less good. It was a work in progress.

"Did you know that Amira now has two little girls?" said Thomas over coffee.

"What?" said Gabriel.

"The little girls she looked after in Eraldus," said Thomas. "Their parents are separated. Amira has them at her house during the week, and the mother has them over the weekend in the family home they have always lived in. I believe it's not far from here."

"Yes, it's quite close,' said Gabriel, recalling where that family lived.

He sat there for a few minutes, trying to make sense of what Thomas had told him.

"How are things with Kathleen?" Gabriel asked, remembering that, on his last visit, Thomas had explained how happy and grateful he was that he and Kathleen had reconnected.

"It's been a year of seeing each other again," said Thomas. "It started slowly, but I probably see her most weeks now. She still won't come to Waldmeer, but I think we are making headway in rebuilding some trust."

"What do you think happened?" asked Gabriel, who was more

interested in relationship failures and successes generally than Thomas's particular case.

Sensing this, Thomas said, "Have you not noticed that although we put enormous value on our couple relationships, they are minefields of hurt and betrayal, both real and imagined?"

Gabriel was listening. Thomas got into teaching mode. His teaching style had improved this year. It had a greater depth from hard-earned life experience and practising what he was preaching.

"Have you not noticed how much lying we do in them?" said Thomas honestly. "We tell ourselves it's not lies, or if it is, it is excusable for self-defence purposes. How little we realise that every lie digs us deeper into a painful delusion, and we end up building war zones, not love boats."

TOUCHED

CHAPTER 39
MISS YOU

Amira was admiring a different generation of sweet peas. This lot was winding up the footpath railing and onto the front doorsteps. They seemed to be singing a soft, repetitive song.

Tell him you miss him. Tell him you miss him.

After a while, Amira caught on and replied, "No, I won't."

Tell him you miss him.

"No, he's married."

Tell him you miss him.

"His partner will get upset with me if I tell him that."

Tell him you miss him.

"He doesn't care if I miss him or not."

Tell him you miss him.

Amira sighed and picked a couple of pretty sweet peas. It was pointless not to do as they wished—"they" being what was behind the sweet peas. She went inside, placed the flowers between two bits of paper, and put them in the middle of a heavy book.

A few days later, she took them out, and they had turned into pressed flowers. She carefully slid them into an envelope with a note saying, *I miss you.* She addressed the envelope to Gabriel, put it in the mailbox on the corner, and said to the wind, *I hope they know what they are talking about.*

CHAPTER 40
COURTING

Teresa and Bryan were going well. Well enough that, long ago, Teresa introduced Bryan to her girls. He only stayed overnight when the girls were with their father in the city, but he was a frequent day visitor when the girls were home. Teresa was conscious of protecting her girl's interests and not stressing them with a new family member. She was equally intent on keeping Bryan as her boyfriend. As he was relatively young and didn't have children, she felt he needed time to adjust to the demands of two girls in their early teens. She was realistic about step-parenting. It is hard enough for parents to come to terms with the unselfishness required for children, let alone step-parents who do not have the biological and emotional attachment to the child. Adjustment time on both sides and low expectations seemed the best approach. Teresa did her very best to make it all work.

Overall, it was working, with only minor problems now and again. However, after all her careful work, a bull had been let loose in the china shop. The girls had inadvertently let their father know about Bryan, and he was furious. Arthur was intelligent, vindictive, and unhappy—the right combination to create trouble in other people's lives. Further, he was an astute liar who always convinced himself that he was speaking the truth. He prided himself on his high ethics. Teresa did not take his trouble-making lightly. That would have been foolish. She did not tell Bryan anything about it as she didn't want to burden him. Anyway, she felt Arthur was a problem she had invited into her own life, so it was up to her to deal with him. Although she was correct about Arthur, she underestimated Bryan.

A solicitor's letter arrived saying that Arthur would fight for sole custody of the girls because their mother was providing "an unsuitable and unstable environment due to her young male companions." He said that he was better equipped to raise them. Teresa knew that Arthur did not really want the girls—he was far too busy, and they would end up on their own for long periods—but he would employ the best lawyers. He was a convincing actor and would present well in court. Teresa worried that, in comparison, she might come across as less than marvellous. Besides, no matter how she came across, she knew the impact a powerful, wealthy, and determined man could have in any situation.

Teresa was angry, but more than that, she was scared. This would have an enormous effect on her girl's well-being. She tried to reassure herself that although Arthur had the fire of vindictiveness, she had the fire of a mother's love.

CHAPTER 41
GIRL-BED

The girls and Amira sat at the round kitchen table, having dinner. The dusk had receded, and it was getting dark, but Amira hadn't bothered to close the curtains. In Waldmeer, it didn't matter.

Two headlights appeared not far from the window. They all wondered who it was. The girls ran outside, eager for any visitor. However, when they saw it was a man they didn't know, they quickly ran back inside.

It was Gabriel.

After Amira waved to him, the girls deemed it safe and decided to follow him down to the bungalow. He didn't send them away. With the openness of children, they would stay with him for as long as he allowed.

About fifteen minutes later, the three of them appeared at the back door of the main house.

"There's water all over the bungalow," said Marilyn, anxious to report the news.

"Oh no," said Amira. "Is there a leak?"

"Yes," said Gabriel. "It's above the bed. My art stuff is fine, but the bed is wet."

They all went to investigate, and Amira brought a bucket. There was no room to move the bed, so Gabriel lifted it onto its side. He guessed where the leak was coming from and put the bucket there.

"I'll fix it later," he said.

Amira was not as confident in Gabriel's handyman skills as he was, but said, "Sure," not wanting to dampen his enthusiasm.

"I told Gabriel that he can have my room tonight, and I'll sleep in with Marilyn," said Bianca, wanting to keep their visitor longer.

The girls missed their Dad. Amira looked at Gabriel, who wasn't objecting.

"If he doesn't mind sleeping in a girl-bed," she said.

Gabriel smiled at Amira and said, "I have done that before."

And that was the first of Gabriel's staying in the girl-bed, which happened numerous times over the coming months. He kept saying he would fix the roof, but needed to find out how. He didn't seem in any great hurry.

ON ONE OF Gabriel's visits, Amira asked him about Paul.

"We separated six months ago," said Gabriel.

Amira was surprised that he hadn't already told her.

"I didn't want to be part of the divorce statistic," said Gabriel, "but now I am. Because we were married less than two years, we had to go to a counselling session."

"How was that?" asked Amira.

"Terrible. Painful."

Gabriel looked disgusted with the whole thing and said, "Never again."

Amira wasn't sure if he meant never again for marriage or

never again for divorce, but assumed both by the look on Gabriel's face.

"How is Paul?" she asked, feeling that Paul would be suffering more from the whole process.

"He'll be fine," said Gabriel. "He'll find someone else."

CHAPTER 42
TOY BOY

"What the hell?" said Bryan.

Teresa had never seen him even close to this angry.

"You thought you would keep the whole thing about Arthur and the court case to yourself? Why, in God's name, would you do that? Do you think I am incapable—a child?"

He added sarcastically, "In case you haven't noticed, I'm a grown man."

"Of course, you are," said Teresa, "but...."

"Don't you trust me? Do you respect me so little? What else haven't you told me?" he demanded. "What else?"

"You're being silly," said Teresa quietly.

Bryan was in no mood for correction.

"I thought we were in this together," he said. "Obviously, not. Am I some sort of toy boy that's good for fun but not much else?"

Toy boy was a word Teresa never said around Bryan because she thought it was insulting to both.

"Am I just a rebound from Arthur," said Bryan, "to amuse you for a while when your girls aren't around?"

Holding her face in his hands, he said, "You have no intention of having a serious relationship with me, do you?"

He grabbed his jacket and slammed the door.

Neither Teresa nor Bryan slept much that night. The girls were in the city with their father, so Teresa's flat was particularly empty. It was above the Waldmeer bookshop and overlooked the main beach. She opened the balcony door at 4.00 a.m. The breeze off the water was fresh. The sky was a mixture of clouds, stars, and a half-formed moon, which sporadically appeared between the clouds as if to remind anyone watching that it may be hidden but was not absent. Although Teresa was very upset about the argument and worried it might be their last one, she could not help feeling a little pleased that Bryan cared about being in her life that much. On that partially comforting note, she went back to bed to get an hour or two of sleep.

She didn't contact Bryan over the coming days because she felt that if he was going to return, he had to do so when he was ready. It only took two days. Bryan was a straightforward person. He didn't dwell on things. He said what he wanted, and troubles would fade from his mind without consciously trying. This trouble didn't exactly *fade from his mind,* but the anger did and was replaced with an idea. When Teresa opened the door and saw it was Bryan, tears came to her eyes. She wasn't one to cry in front of people. She spent too long in a fragmented marriage to do that. Bryan hugged her, and they only reluctantly let go of each other. They sat on the balcony together, drinking herbal tea.

"I have an idea," said Bryan. "I think we should get engaged."

Teresa spat out her tea. Bryan knew she would be unprepared, so he didn't take offence. He even laughed.

When Teresa realised he was serious, she took his hand and said softly, "Bryan, I love you. It's that simple. But you haven't had your children yet, and I wouldn't take that away from you."

Teresa may not have been prepared for this discussion, but Bryan was.

"I think," he said, "we have already discussed the point of my being quite capable of making my own decisions."

"Yes, we have," said Teresa, smiling.

"It might help with the court case for you to have a stable relationship," said Bryan.

"And you may feel more willing to share the girls with me," he added hopefully. "Regardless, I want to marry you."

He looked towards the ocean. It was so familiar to him.

"You have had a far more interesting life than I," he continued. "I have only ever lived here. But I don't need to live anywhere else to know what I want. I don't think you are ready to marry me at this stage, but if we get engaged, I don't care how long it takes you to get there."

Teresa was truly stunned by Bryan's maturity. She felt embarrassed to have not seen it before, but told herself that maybe it wasn't there before.

It is there now, she thought. *Right now, he is more of a teacher than any kind of a "toy". I guess that's what love does. Those we love become our teachers, whether we intend it or not.*

HOPE

CHAPTER 43
OPPORTUNITY

Teresa had eight big bags lined up. They were full of her rich clothes from the years with Arthur. Two by two, she took the bags down the stairs, past her bookshop, to the Op Shop a few doors away.

When the shop assistant started unpacking them and saw the expensive brand names, she said kindly, "Are you sure you want to give us all these beautiful clothes, dear? They've hardly been worn."

The manager, who was in the Country Women's Association with Teresa's mother, entered from the backroom and said, "I see you are having a big clean-up. *A clean-up is as good as a holiday.*"

Teresa smiled at her misquoting the saying that *a change is as good as a holiday,* but thought that a clean-up was as good as a change, and both were as good as a holiday.

～

"THAT'S the daughter of the Hemingways," said the shop manager to the assistant when they were both in the back room. "She left

Waldmeer years ago to marry an older man—a tycoon. It didn't work out, and now she's back in Waldmeer with her daughters."

"Oh, is that who she is?" said the other woman.

"I heard she is now engaged to Bryan, Clarice's youngest child," said the shop manager. "They are the farm next to the Hemingways. Teresa would have known him when he was a child."

"She's gone from gold digger to cougar," said the other woman.

"Amelia!" the shop manager scolded, but also smiled in good-natured amusement.

"Don't you worry," said Amelia mischievously. "Who wants money when you can have fun?"

The shop manager slapped her wrist and said, "Well, keep away from my sons. And half your luck if you find someone else."

CHAPTER 44
REBORN

Teresa's eldest daughter, Josephine, and Ide's eldest son, Christopher, were both fourteen and in the same year level at Waldmeer State Secondary School. The two mothers usually sat together at school meetings and functions. Their mutual connection to Amira cemented their friendship, but it had its own flavour.

When the three women were together or when Amira was with either of them separately, conversations took the path that Amira designated. Amira didn't mind the topic, but she did mind the direction of any conversation. If either of the women had a problem and wanted to discuss it, Amira was more than happy to let them express their feelings. However, she would not allow conversations to deteriorate into complaining, blaming, gossiping or laughing at other people's expense. When it came to the general public, Amira would quickly exit destructive or pointless conversations. However, if her *trusted ones* were the conversationalists, she would correct them and then exit the conversation.

Ide and Teresa were both very aware of this and sometimes

laughed to each other that they just needed to have a good old bitch.

"Don't go to Amira if you want to bitch," they would say to each other. "You'll get a lecture."

They only ever trusted each other with Amira-jokes because they knew their loyalty to her was unquestioned. Away from Amira and within the safety of their friendship, they sometimes took the opportunity to bitch, laugh, and complain about life as much as they wanted. Not only would it not be repeated, but most of the time, it was not even taken seriously. Teresa's favourite topic of complaint was Arthur. Ide oscillated between the hospital matron and Farkas, although she loved the latter and not the former.

Lately, whenever Ide, Teresa, and their children were together, Christopher took his baby brother off Ide's lap, carried him over to Josephine, and presented her with the baby. Josephine was always thrilled, and they would play with the baby for as long as the circumstances would allow. Christopher was not an average type of fourteen-year-old boy, although he was well-liked by his peers. He was a creative soul and a searching thinker. He was more interested in people than in any of the things that his male peers were interested in. While his peers treated girls as some sort of annoying but captivating entity to somehow be organised into submission, Christopher saw them as people—interesting, intelligent, and of value to his being.

"Have you noticed how close Christopher and Josephine are becoming?" Ide said to Teresa.

"Yes, I have," said Teresa.

Both women watched the two young friends playing with the baby.

"Love never fails to save the world," said Teresa.

"It keeps getting reborn," said Ide.

"Love or the world?" asked Teresa.

"Both," replied Ide.

CHAPTER 45
THE LIST

"I was going to ring you," said Teresa as Amira entered the bookshop. "I have the most wonderful news."

"Yes, I know," said Amira, smiling. "You're engaged. You already told me."

Teresa rolled her eyes.

"No, seriously, I have big news about your manuscript. Someone from Hope Publishing in the States rang this morning and is interested in it."

"Really?" said Amira in surprise.

Last year, once her house in Eraldus was sold, Amira started to write newsletters for her clients in the city. She didn't have the girls to attend to as she did now, and the number of clients she saw in Waldmeer was relatively few. Waldmeer was, after all, a small, coastal village. Healers were hardly the first port of call for most of its residents.

As she had time on her hands, Amira spent it in her garden or writing the letters. They became longer and more frequent. By the end of the year, she had enough of them to edit together into a book. She printed, bound, and sent it to her city clients as a present. Teresa was listed as author-agent. She wasn't an agent, but she *was* willing and a bookshop owner.

At the time, Amira told Teresa, "We will both be in this together. It will be the blind leading the blind or, more fortuitously, companion adventurers."

"One of your city clients gave the manuscript to her brother, who was visiting from the States," said Teresa. "He loved it and gave it to his friend at Hope Publishing. They are one of the biggest self-help publishers. They said they want you to travel to Los Angeles and sign a book contract if all goes well. You would need to live there some of the year to promote the book and future ones."

Teresa stared wide-eyed at Amira and said, "This is every author's dream. If they publish you, you could end up on the New York Times Best Seller list."

Amira was silent.

"Here is their number," continued Teresa. "Ring them today."

As Amira turned for the door, still having said nothing, Teresa added, "One more thing. His last words to me were, 'We need a new guru. Several of our bestselling ones have died. I think your author may fit the bill. She's strange enough to be interesting, sincere enough to be believed, and lives in an exotic enough location to fascinate our U.S. readership. She's sellable, and our job is selling. We believe we have a match.'"

Still trying to get some response from Amira, Teresa said, "This is an offer you can't refuse."

"No, I suppose not," said Amira.

Once Amira had closed the shop door, Teresa thought, *They sure got the "strange" bit right.*

PEACE

CHAPTER 46
REUNION

"Why are you here, Amira?" asked Thomas. "This is not your year level."

It was the ten-year reunion of Maria-Amira's graduating class. Everyone was now twenty-eight. The problem was that although Maria would have been twenty-eight, Amira had gained twelve years in terms of biology and demeanour during her Homeland transition more than two years ago. That made her forty, around the same age as Gabriel and Charlie. It's not that she looked forty. She had a relatively ageless appearance. However, her demeanour was certainly not that of a younger adult. She was told in the Homeland that those who had previously known her would gradually forget how old she was supposed to be and relate to her as she was now. That is exactly what happened. Understandably, Amira was reluctant to go to the reunion and remind everyone of her birth age, but as she lived in Waldmeer, she had no viable excuse not to go.

"This is my correct year level," said Amira.

Thomas looked confused, but then told himself that he had

been there so long that it all rolled into one, and he didn't think about it again.

One of those attending was Mary, Charlie's partner of the last five years. Charlie didn't come. Mary took the opportunity to visit her parents, Grace and Joe. Mary's twin brother, Harry, was also there. Harry had been a bully at school and afterwards. Charlie had been the brunt of his and his mates' jokes for many years.

"Wow, a blast from the past," Harry said to Amira. "I haven't seen you for ages. I must tell you that I had a crush on you once you sorted me out about bullying Charlie."

Amira smiled and recalled how he would occasionally send anonymous flowers to her mother's cafe for her. She would recognise his handwriting from school.

"What are you doing these days?" asked Amira.

"I went to university and did teaching," said Harry. "I work in the city at one of the state secondary schools."

"It's a rough area, but they say I'm okay with the kids," he said in an understated, country-boy way.

Amira surmised that he would be terrific with the kids, having just the right combination of toughness, no-nonsense authority, and understanding wrought from personal experience.

"That's wonderful. Congratulations," said Amira.

They both knew she meant, *Congratulations on coming such a long way from the bullying idiot you once were.*

Harry then looked at Amira intently.

"It's peculiar," he said. "You always seemed so young and innocent, but now I look at you, and you seem more like my mother."

Amira laughed and said, "Thanks, Harry. You look great, too."

CHAPTER 47
DEAR DAD

Teresa's girls had not long left for school. She usually waved them off from the balcony, and then they had an idyllic walk along the sea path and up the hill. The fresh ocean air could sweep away a substantial part of a schoolgirl's cares before the day even started.

Before opening the shop, Teresa attended to some housework. As she vacuumed Josephine's floor, she noticed a pile of paper in the waste paper bin. It looked like many drafts of something. She could see that one of the papers on the top was a letter addressed to Josephine's father. Not one to overstep the boundaries of a teenage girl, Teresa nevertheless looked more closely at the letter. Due to the escalating court troubles she was having with Arthur, she wanted to ensure he was not manipulating the girls with false information or intimidation. In this particular case, he wasn't. It was Josephine who initiated the letter. Teresa sat down and read the draft.

Dear Dad,

I hope you don't mind me writing to you. I have a friend (not a boyfriend, Dad) named Christopher. Last weekend, I went with him to see some of his relatives in the back hills of Waldmeer. The relatives are called Clinkers. They are a bit like gypsies. Don't worry. They aren't going to steal me. Christopher told me that the main guy, who runs the ceremonies, is magic. He can see things. I'm not sure what. Christopher doesn't know, either. After the ceremony, I asked the magic man if he could see anything in me. I thought he would say no, but he didn't. He said, "One day, you will be influential in the financial world. You must pay attention to your studies as you will need them. You must remember to be brave and live by your highest beliefs, as that will give you success. You chose your mother and father because you need your mother's emotional intelligence and your father's business acumen to fulfil your function. Also, you will learn from your father's mistakes." Sorry about that last bit. I haven't told Mum, but I thought I would tell you because it would be nice if we could all be friends, seeing as I picked you both.

Love from your daughter, Josephine.

Teresa sat on the bed, holding the draft. She was shaken for numerous reasons. Finance was probably the last field she wanted her daughter to enter after her experience with Arthur. However, more than that, she suddenly felt that the fighting was irrelevant to what mattered. With all Arthur's faults, he still had good qualities. Otherwise, why would she ever have married him? And regardless, Josephine had apparently chosen him for good and bad. It was, indeed, sobering.

She never mentioned the letter to Josephine, and Josephine never mentioned it to her. Teresa was unsure if she ever mailed a final version to her father. However, Teresa's attitude to Arthur had significantly softened. She no longer felt the anger that had been welling up inside her for months. It had disintegrated. Replacing it was a sense that everything could work out without anyone being hurt. For whatever reason, Teresa never received another letter from Arthur's lawyers. No one ever spoke about the court case or getting sole custody again. The whole thing vanished into thin air as if it had never even existed.

CHAPTER 48
CUDDLE

The following weekend, Teresa walked with Bryan at the beach and tried to explain how her feelings towards Arthur had changed. She couldn't mention the letter because that was an issue of Josephine's privacy. However, as Bryan had made it clear that he wanted her to share her life, she tried to talk about what had happened. Bryan could tell that the anger towards Arthur had been replaced with understanding and perhaps even some affection. He said all the right things, but the conversation remained with him uneasily. He started to worry that Teresa might reconnect with Arthur. Although he knew it was unlikely, he couldn't stop the stream of thought.

I can't compete with him, thought Bryan. *He's used to winning.*

Over the next few weeks, Bryan started to withdraw from Teresa. Usually, he slept at her flat and then travelled to the family farm early each morning. However, he was increasingly staying at the farm overnight. He told her that the days there were so long at the moment that he needed to be there at the crack of dawn. Teresa felt him pulling away, but couldn't do anything about it. It scared her. It scared her differently from what Arthur's court case had done. Arthur scared her into protecting her children. This was scaring her deep within her being.

Of course, Clarice was delighted to have her son back. She would make little comments like, "You always have your room here if things don't quite go to plan. Sometimes things happen for a reason."

Bryan would get angry with her and walk outside.

One morning before opening the bookshop, Teresa called into the Op Shop. She could see that her rich clothes were fast disappearing.

"We have lots of happy customers who love the clothes you brought in," said the shop manager.

"That's terrific," said Teresa. "I'm glad they are feeling loved."

Sensing that Teresa looked a little glum, the shop manager said, "How's that young man of yours?"

Teresa responded to her motherliness, saying, "Actually, not that good. He's back home a lot. I think he doesn't trust me."

"Of course he does, dear," said the shop manager, "but, you know, when we put our heart into a relationship, we are very vulnerable. We make up things because the other person has so much power to hurt us. Be patient and let him know that you love him. He'll sort it out himself."

The shop manager saw Clarice at the Country Women's Association monthly meeting that evening. She knew that Clarice would be elated at having her precious Bryan back home.

After the meeting, she handed Clarice some cake and said as if it had only just entered her mind, "We have been fortunate with our marriages, haven't we? They require a lot of give and take over the years, but we both still have our marriages, and they are very respectable, if I do say so myself. We can only hope that our children have the same good fortune."

Clarice ate her cake in silence.

The next afternoon, Bryan called into the bookshop just before closing.

"I'll make dinner tonight," he said.

Trying not to look surprised, Teresa said, "Great."

"And then we can have an early night," said Bryan.

He must be staying the night, thought Teresa.

"That sounds lovely," she said.

"Maybe, even have a bit of a cuddle," said Bryan, smiling.

Teresa then knew he was back. She didn't know why he was back. She didn't care why. She was simply relieved.

That night, after their *bit of a cuddle,* Bryan turned out the bedside lamp and said in the dark, "This morning, my mother said something very peculiar to me."

"What did she say?" asked Teresa.

"She said that although she loved having me home," said Bryan, "you probably missed me and that as she wasn't the number one woman in my life anymore, I should be getting back to you before you run off with someone else."

Teresa was more stunned than Bryan had been.

Bryan pulled her to him and said, "I don't want you to run off with someone else, but if you ever did, it would have still been all worth it. I would not regret a single instant."

He rolled over and fell into a peaceful sleep. So did Teresa.

FAME

CHAPTER 49
WORDS

Gabriel had started dating again, male and female. He didn't sleep with any of them. These days, he was too old to imagine that one could sleep with another person without paying the price. He wasn't willing to pay that price, so he didn't.

Amira told him about her upcoming trip to Los Angeles. It would soon be the school holidays. She was going to take Marilyn and Bianca to the States so they could see their father.

"My Eraldus lease is coming up for renewal," said Gabriel when next he was in Waldmeer.

Since Paul moved out, there was only Gabriel in the house.

"The house is too expensive for me," he continued, "but I don't have any clear idea of where to go next."

"The girls and I will be gone by next weekend," said Amira, "and we'll be away for a month. Why don't you stay here for the month?"

With no better alternative, Gabriel agreed.

Besides briefly telling him about her trip, Amira hadn't mentioned much else because he didn't want to discuss it. She left her manuscript on the lounge room table so he could look at it if he wanted.

"Have you had a look at my book?" asked Amira.

"I hate reading. You know that," said Gabriel.

He tried reading the first chapter but didn't even reach the bottom of the first page. Another time, he tried another chapter. He didn't do much better. He read it at night when everyone was asleep. He was a night person. Amira was a morning person.

"I looked at it," said Gabriel one morning, not explaining what he had looked at.

Amira knew what it was.

"And? Do you like it?" she asked.

"No. I don't understand it," said Gabriel. "The words are too big."

He said it as if it were the fault of the words that were being difficult to get along with.

"And the ideas are too complicated," he complained.

Gabriel spoke dismissively because he didn't like Amira's new life direction, though there was some truth in what he said.

CHAPTER 50
ON THE LINE

A few weeks passed with Gabriel living in Waldmeer. This morning, he stood behind Farkas at the baker's. They nodded to each other as men do. Ide and the baby had softened Farkas. He was more settled, although *settled* and *Farkas* didn't quite go together.

"You at Amira's while she is in the States?" asked Farkas.

"Yep," said Gabriel.

"What do you think about Amira's book contract?" he added after a pause.

Farkas looked surprised that his opinion was being sought and answered, "She was always going to do well."

"Yeah?" said Gabriel.

"I have known her for a long time," said Farkas.

"How long?" asked Gabriel, realising he had no idea how Farkas and Amira first met.

Farkas paused and said, "Longer than I can remember."

"I remember you knew her already when I first met her at Waldmeer Corner Store and Cafe," said Gabriel.

"Back then, she was just a girl," said Farkas. "Not anymore."

Farkas smiled and continued, "You have to be brave to take her on now. I'm brave. Not that brave."

"I don't think so," said Gabriel.

"Don't think what?" said Farkas. "That I'm not that brave or that she is trouble?"

Gabriel didn't reply. He didn't want to enter either of those conversations.

Farkas's face relaxed.

"She is not the sort of person that can be controlled," he said.

Gabriel shrugged as if it were of no relevance to him.

"She doesn't even control herself," said Farkas.

Gabriel glanced towards the counter to see how far the line had progressed, and said, "Oh my God, this line is ridiculous. It hasn't even moved."

He left.

There was only one person in front of Farkas.

CHAPTER 51
UNNECESSARY

In the US:

A few days before Amira was due to return home from the States, she received a phone call from Marilyn and Bianca's father, Peter. Amira thought he would be ringing to confirm where he would meet her at the airport so she could collect the girls.

"Hi, Pete. How are you?" said Amira.

"We're all good, thanks," said Peter brightly.

Amira surmised that his time with the girls must have gone well.

"I'm glad," she said.

"I'm ringing to let you know I will be returning home on the same flight as you," said Peter.

Home? thought Amira. *I thought here was home now.*

"I might as well tell you," said Peter, "because it will affect your life as well as ours. I'm going to try to work things out with Melissa."

"Okay," said Amira. "I hope it does work out."

IN ERALDUS:

Peter and Melissa were sitting at an outside table at the Eraldus cafe.

"It feels good to be back," said Peter. "Thanks for coming to talk with me. How are the girls after their long flight?"

"Exhausted," said Melissa. "They are still asleep."

She looked at Peter, who was fidgeting in an uncustomary fashion. He had always held most of the cards in their marriage.

"They said they had a lovely time with you," said Melissa.

Peter smiled and lightened a little.

"I forgot about the incomprehensible and unpredictable weather here," he said, pulling up his collar. "Why, on earth, is it cold at this time of the year?"

"Well, you didn't dress appropriately," scolded Melissa in a good-natured way.

"Nonsense!" said Peter. "It's the damn weather that is inappropriate, not me."

Melissa laughed and was happy to hear one of his old jokes. Somehow, it seemed funny again. Nothing he had said for the last year seemed even remotely funny.

After their breakfast and a chat about incidental things, Melissa stood up. Peter watched her. He had not mentioned anything about his plan to return.

"Well, I think the girls will be awake by now," said Melissa. "They have become so used to seeing you every day that you'd better walk home with me so they can talk to you."

After paying, they headed for home. Peter brushed a finger against Melissa's hand. He was terrified that she would pull away. It was one of the most important and frightening moments of his life.

She put her hand in his and said nothing. In fact, nothing was ever said about Peter's time in the States or his return to Melissa.

It was not necessary.

CHAPTER 52
STORY

In Waldmeer:

Although Gabriel enjoyed having the house to himself, he missed Amira. He missed her more because he didn't know how much she would even be in Waldmeer in the future. He got a lot of work done without the distractions of the city. He was pleased with that, less pleased with himself. Reluctant to admit it, he was affected by his conversation with Farkas.

Everything seems fine, thought Gabriel, *and then things start unravelling on their own for no rational reason.*

He decided to be more honest. After all, no one could hear him but himself.

Who am I kidding? I push Amira away, myself. It's easy to be nice to people who don't mean that much to us. But if something matters to us, we will fight to make it work in our favour. Do we even know what is in our favour?

He walked outside and listened to the faint sounds of the sea at the bottom of the hill. He watched the kookaburras eyeing him off. Yesterday, one of them swooped down and grabbed a whole sandwich out of his hand. Their beaks are strong.

"You won't get me again, you thief," yelled Gabriel. "You missed my face by one centimetre!"

"I HAVE SOMETHING FOR YOU," said Amira the following evening.

She quickly unpacked and took a pile of papers, clipped together, from her bag.

"Another book," groaned Gabriel. "I don't want it. I didn't even like the first one."

"It's not a book," said Amira, undeterred by Gabriel's off-hand manner. "It's only two chapters."

She left it on the kitchen bench, knowing that if he were going to read it, it would be late at night.

THE NEXT DAY, Amira said, "You haven't asked me about my trip or the children. Haven't you noticed they are not here?"

"Yes, of course, I noticed," said Gabriel. "I assumed they were still in the city."

"Peter and Melissa are most likely reuniting," said Amira, "and the children will return to their old Eraldus school. They won't be here anymore."

Gabriel looked at Amira. She seemed somewhat sad. She probably liked having the girls because she didn't have her own children.

"Oh, I'm sorry," he said. "But it's for the best. They need to be with their parents."

"Yes," said Amira, who always knew their stay was temporary.

"You still have me," said Gabriel.

Amira smiled and said, "Bianca doesn't need her room anymore, so you are welcome to it for as long as you want."

"I'm returning to Eraldus this afternoon to deal with some work," said Gabriel. "I'll stay with a friend. I'll be back in a few days."

When he was leaving, he said, "Your new book is a story. I read it last night."

"Yes, it is. Did you understand it better than my other book?" asked Amira.

"Yes, I did," said Gabriel.

"And?" asked Amira.

"It made me think, but at least I knew what I was supposed to be thinking about," said Gabriel.

"And?" asked Amira again.

"I've had a whole month of thinking," said Gabriel. "Way too much thinking for me."

He hugged her goodbye and said, "See you in two days."

CHAPTER 53
UNRECOGNISABLE

I*n the Leleks:*

The forest was shining with soft, wavering light. It was a pristine, sacred morning.

Perfect, thought Amira.

Although she had seen Erdo a few times in town during the last two years, she had not driven out to see him in the Leleks since before her Eraldus days. Erdo was waiting on the other side of the old walking bridge. Amira saw two splendid black swans on the lake and wondered if it was the same pair she had often seen years ago.

"Yes, it is," said Erdo. "Swans mate for life, although sometimes they part if nesting fails. Otherwise, they work with the bond they've made."

Amira sat on a decaying tree trunk and watched the lake, which always seemed to have a special enchantment.

After about ten minutes, she said, "I haven't told anyone yet, but I didn't sign the book contract."

Erdo nodded.

"The first two weeks in the States were a whirlwind of meetings, interviews, bookstores, lawyers, and experts," said Amira.

One of the swans suddenly departed, but the mate stayed. Amira waited to see what would happen next. Nothing happened, so she continued.

"I hated it," she said. "I hated every minute of it."

"Is that why you didn't sign?" asked Erdo.

"I started to dream of Alamgir," said Amira. "I kept expecting to see him, but I never did. I'd know that dark malevolence anywhere. I was a little anxious that I might see him here today as I did one other time."

Erdo put his hands in the air and pointed at the tranquil surroundings to indicate he was not there.

"They organised a whole month of engagements for me," explained Amira, "but I'd made my decision before two weeks were up. I told them that I wasn't their guru. They were rather stunned and tried to talk me out of it. When they couldn't, they aborted mission and returned my manuscript. That was the last I heard of them. After that, I spent a few days wandering—beaches, parks, streets. I tried not to think about anything in particular."

The swan returned, and its mate swam over and circled it with effortless fluidity. It was all grace and poise.

"And then," said Amira, "I started to write something new, something different—a story. So, I knew it was the right decision."

"I'm an old hermit who lives away from the world. I know nothing of publishing," said Erdo.

"Yes, but you have sources," said Amira. "Inside information."

"It was the right decision," said Erdo. "The seduction of success and fame is great and treacherous."

He wandered over to the lake and threw a stick into the middle of the water. He watched as the rings spread to the edge.

"And what of Alamgir?" asked Amira. "I still haven't seen him, and he always comes to me if I start dreaming of him."

"Oh, you saw him," said Erdo. "You saw him many times when you were away. You just didn't recognise him."

CHAPTER 54
FURTHER

"I'm sorry that it didn't work out how you wanted," said Amira to Teresa. "It might be every author's dream, but I don't dream about such things."

"Do it your way," said Teresa in a resigned manner. "However, I do wish we had something we could give people. Right now, we have nothing."

"We have hope," said Amira. "A hope that will not delude or deceive and will include everyone and disadvantage no one."

Teresa nodded.

"I may not have dreams of fame," said Amira, "but I dream for the world."

Teresa ran her hand along one of the shelves as if trying to make something more concrete materialise in her safe, little corner of the world.

Amira touched her hand and said, "And we have these."

She pulled five books out of her bag. In her last two weeks in the States, Amira had her manuscript made into some paperbacks without the help of the publishers.

Given something more tangible, Teresa's expression gladdened. She took the books and created a space on the shelf.

Looking up at Amira hopefully, she said, "We have all come this far together. Together, we can go further."

SUMMARY OF WALDMEER SERIES

A multi-generational journey of spiritual awakening, healing, and the spaces between worlds.

Beneath the surface of an idyllic coastal village, unseen forces stir. Waldmeer is a place where the visible and invisible meet—where inter-dimensional realms brush against everyday life, and where emotional truths rise quietly but undeniably.

Told across seven books, the *Waldmeer Series* follows Maria–Amira from the groundedness of her rural home to the doorways into higher realms of perception and spiritual transformation. Around her, those she loves and seeks to help are drawn into their own awakenings, resistances, and reckonings.

Waldmeer moves between ordinary moments and other-worldly initiations. Between earthly love and higher love. Between who we think we are... and what we truly are.

At times tender, at times confronting, these stories unfold in layers—personal, relational, and metaphysical.

ABOUT THE AUTHOR

On the beach at Lorne, Australia (the coastal village Waldmeer is based on).

Donna Goddard is a spiritual author whose work blends clarity, devotion, and metaphysical insight. With more than twenty published books across spiritual nonfiction, fiction, poetry, and children's literature, she writes to uplift consciousness and offer healing through words.

Donna's Facebook author page has over 400,000 followers worldwide, and her YouTube channel has received 4 million views. Her books are read by spiritual seekers globally and are known for their honesty, poetic style, and transformative energy.

Her writing is an offering—to help others awaken their own inner spirit, trust its guidance, and create a life of depth, beauty, and quiet joy.

All links at https://linktr.ee/donnagoddard

Ratings and Reviews

Donna would be grateful for any ratings or reviews.

ALSO BY DONNA GODDARD

Fiction
Waldmeer Series: A Spiritual Fiction Series
Nanima Series: Spiritual Fiction
Enanika Series: Visionary Fiction
Riverland Series (children's fiction 6 to 9 years)
Foxie (children's fiction 7 to 12 years)

Nonfiction
Love and Devotion Series
Sweet Spirit Series
Consciousness Series
Meditation Series
Poetry Series
Love's Longing
Dance: A Spiritual Affair
Writing: A Spiritual Voice

www.ingramcontent.com/pod-product-compliance
Lightning Source LLC
Chambersburg PA
CBHW060817120726
47909CB00006B/1964